KU-023-300

Blade and Bone

CATHERINE JOHNSON

WALKER BOOKS

Blade and Bone

For Adam Catlin, without whom I would never
have met Ezra – or rather Ezra's tumour in a jar –
in the Hunterian Museum, London

This is a work of fiction. Names, characters, places and incidents
are either the product of the author's imagination or, if real, used
fictitiously. All statements, activities, stunts, descriptions, information
and material of any other kind contained herein are included for
entertainment purposes only and should not be relied on for
accuracy or replicated as they may result in injury.

First published 2016 by Walker Books Ltd
87 Vauxhall Walk, London SE11 5HJ

2 4 6 8 10 9 7 5 3 1

Text © 2016 Catherine Johnson
Cover illustration © 2016 Royston Knipe

The right of Catherine Johnson to be identified as author of this
work has been asserted by her in accordance with the
Copyright, Designs and Patents Act 1988

This book has been typeset in Adobe Caslon

Printed and bound in Great Britain by Clays Ltd, St Ives plc

All rights reserved. No part of this book may be reproduced,
transmitted or stored in an information retrieval system in any
form or by any means, graphic, electronic or mechanical,
including photocopying, taping and recording, without prior
written permission from the publisher.

British Library Cataloguing in Publication Data:
a catalogue record for this book is available from the British Library

ISBN 978-1-4063-4187-4

www.walker.co.uk

McAdam's Anatomy School and Museum of Curiosities
Great Windmill Street
Soho
London
1 March 1793

M. Bichat,

I am writing in regard to the kind Invitation you
extended to me when we met last year at my
Master's funeral. I do hope this is still open — that is,
to visit your Famous & Most respected Hospital, the
Hôtel-Dieu in Paris. My own Affairs mean I will be in
Paris later this month.

It would be an excellent Opportunity to meet with
you again, and to see for myself the Experiments and
Medical Advancements you spoke of. As my Business is
urgent, I must leave immediately, and will not receive
any Correspondence sent to London. However, I will
call on you when I arrive in Paris. I look forward to
seeing you and the esteemed Monsieur Figaud once
more.

I assure you, I am aware of the trouble between
our two countries, but I hope that we may meet, not
as an Englishman and a Frenchman, but as two men of
science and learning. As brother Surgeons.

  Your colleague,

Ezra McAdam, Surgeon

The Fleur de Lys Tavern
Near Lille
France
6 March 1793

My dear Loveday,

I hope with all my Heart that you are well and that
you might have found Mahmoud — that this journey will
be In Vain. That you and Mahmoud will even now be
laughing as you read this. Indeed, if you set out for
Venice, and for Constantinople, before I arrive, I beg
you leave word at your address that I may return to
London without Anxiety.

I am writing to tell you I am on my way to Paris and
am already in France as I write this Note. Crossing
the Channel was most unpleasant, not least due to the
foul weather. I fear the fellows who conveyed me
were smugglers. I kept my mouth shut and imagined
you would most certainly enjoy my discomfort. We did, at
least, reach France without incident, and the Locals do
not seem for the most part Concerned that I am an
Englishman — all Negroes are "American" here.

However, not all is without Incident. The stagecoach
to Paris broke down en route and I have been
Delayed in the city of Lille, close to the Belgian

border, where there is some kind of War. All is not lost – there is a Regiment of the Revolutionary Army stationed here that has promised me Assistance in my continuing journey in exchange for my expertise as a Surgeon. I am destined with them for the battlefield and once I have stitched up a few of their Soldiers I will be on my way.

I Hope all is well with you and that Mahmoud is safe. There are such lies told about this Revolution on the streets of London. Be sure I have ignored the most of them. I must admit I think it a sign of Great Advancement for any people to want to Govern themselves without the Intercedence of any Kings or Lords or Suchlike. And these soldiers are a great testament to the Rightness of their Cause.

Your friend,

Ezra McAdam

Chapter One

A Farm on the French–Belgian Border
Near Lille
18 March 1793

"Light!" Ezra struggled for the word in French. *"Lumière! Maintenant!"* The boy with the lamp came closer. He could be no more than eleven, and his face was whiter than best Irish linen, his eyes fixed on the soldier on the table. Ezra looked back at his patient.

On the makeshift table, held down by two other soldiers and yelling in French all the oaths known to man, lay an infantryman of the American Regiment of the Revolutionary Army. His coat was thick with mud, and one of his legs was shattered, flesh pulped, shards of bone exploded into white sawdust. He screamed. That was a good sign. He was alive.

Ezra took the bone saw, and as he began to work, the soldier's cries turned from oaths to tears, sobs loud enough to drown out the sound of metal on bone. Ezra was relieved when the pain drove the man to unconsciousness, and it wasn't long before he heard the remains of the leg drop with a soft thud onto the floor of the barn. Then, just as suddenly, the lamp and the boy holding it fell too – the boy had fainted clean away. Ezra cursed and carried on in the dark.

At sixteen years of age Ezra McAdam was already a talented surgeon. He had learned his trade from his master, Mr William McAdam, and had inherited both his home and his practice from the very same man, who had brought him to England from the West Indies as an infant and raised him not as a slave, but as an apprentice. Ezra had honed his skills in London's operating theatres, and he did not feel conceited to hazard that he was among the best in his field. Yet this was no operating theatre, and this was not London but the French countryside; his assistants were soldiers who did not speak English, and his only audience was a couple of goats and an ox that took badly to the smell of blood.

As if it could read Ezra's thoughts, the ox lowed and kicked at his stall. Ezra wiped his brow, and felt for a pulse in his patient.

"Monsieur McAdam!" The door banged open. It was Lieutenant Colonel Dumas, the head of the American Regiment. "Will he live?" Ezra nodded, too exhausted to speak, and the Lieutenant Colonel's face lit up in relief.

At well over six foot, Dumas was the tallest and most dashing young officer in the regiment, and the only one who favoured a moustache. He was also the first military officer Ezra had ever spoken to who was black.

Despite the name, most men of the American Regiment had never actually seen America. In France, Ezra had learnt, "American" was the term for all people of colour, and the regiment comprised men from the

Caribbean as well as French-born soldiers, plus a few actual Americans. There were also ink-dark Africans and almost white quadroons, mulattos of every shade and mixture – all bound together to fight for freedom. Ezra couldn't help being a little swept off his feet.

"I would be honoured, *monsieur*," the Lieutenant Colonel was saying, "if you would stay with the American Regiment – a surgeon of your inestimable skill would make a tremendous difference to us."

Ezra felt a surge of pride. He wanted to say it would be an honour for him, too; he'd seen the aftermath of battle; he knew how much of a difference he might make here. And Lieutenant Colonel Dumas was the kind of man one couldn't help but want to please.

But Ezra hadn't come to France to help the war effort, no matter how much he approved of the revolution. Two weeks ago, he'd been on his way to Paris, his goal to find his friend Loveday Finch and the future Ottoman sultan, Prince Mahmoud, and help set them on their way to Constantinople.

He knew he could be of use to the regiment, but with Mahmoud missing and Loveday stranded in Paris, an English girl alone in France in the midst of the revolution… The longer he kept them waiting, the more uncertain their fates.

In London, he and Loveday had helped the boy prince Mahmoud escape from an Ottoman conspiracy with the Russians, who wanted him dead; the only thing that made Mahmoud safer travelling through Paris than remaining in London was the hope that his pursuers didn't know he was there. Then Loveday had written to tell Ezra that

Mahmoud was missing – and it seemed that hope might be in vain.

"I cannot, sir," he said finally, with regret. "I have friends waiting in Paris who need me."

He had told the lieutenant colonel as much when he had arrived here, after the diligence – the stagecoach – had broken down outside Calais. The regiment had been in a sorry shape after a run-in with the Dutch Army, there'd been a number of men injured and Ezra had offered his assistance in the hope that they might somehow help his make his way onward to Paris. He had been with the regiment for twelve days since then, but so far transport had been hard to find.

"Yes, of course." Dumas's brow creased in a frown. "You know that now Britain is at war with France, it will not be easy for you to travel anywhere." If he had been anyone else, Ezra would have suspected the lieutenant colonel of trying to persuade him not to go. But the thoughtfulness in Dumas's voice was genuine, and Ezra was struck by the feeling that he could trust him.

"Sir, might we speak somewhere in private?" he asked, and Lieutenant Colonel Dumas nodded, and indicated that he should follow him out of the barn into the grey early morning.

They crossed the yard, past the stables, where men and horses were mostly still asleep, making their way towards the farmhouse where the lieutenant colonel and his entourage had billeted themselves. The farmhouse kitchen was low-ceilinged and gloomy. An old woman was building the fire; she looked at them both with narrowed eyes as they passed, doubtless less than pleased to have a regiment of "Americans" occupying her farm, but Dumas seemed not to notice. He led Ezra on into what might have been the drawing room. There was last night's fire still glowing orange, and a couple of officers were asleep where they sat, coats and saddle blankets draped over them like quilts. Ezra stopped. These men had no doctor, nor did the men they commanded. If he stayed he might be able to save so many lives.

Dumas's hand on his shoulder interrupted his thoughts. "I am afraid this may be as private as we will find," he whispered. The sleeping officers showed no sign of stirring.

So Ezra told Dumas the whole story. About Loveday – the brash and spirited magician's daughter who had become his dearest friend and ally – and a little, as much as he dared, about Mahmoud. And then how Ezra had come as soon as he received Loveday's message, from London to Dover and across the sea to Calais.

"My friends may be in danger. Not only because they could be taken for enemies of France – which, I assure you, they are not – but from the Russians, or—" Ezra stopped; he did not wish to reveal too much about Mahmoud, nor the plot to ensure he did not take his place on the Ottoman throne.

Dumas laughed. "The world against a child and a girl?"

Ezra bit his lip. Perhaps he should have stayed silent. But Dumas softened. "You must excuse me. I understand these people are close to your heart." He looked at Ezra thoughtfully. "I have a letter that needs to be delivered to General Le Brun at the War Office in Paris," he said, "requesting supplies and boots for our men. You can take it for me – I cannot leave the regiment."

Ezra felt a wave of relief wash over him, and opened his mouth to thank the man, but the lieutenant colonel held up his hand. "Paris is dangerous, especially for a foreign girl, even if she can handle a sword – you must go quickly. And as to the boy, it will be like searching for a grain of wheat in a sack of barley. But this errand on behalf of the regiment may afford you some protection at least; you will be acting on behalf of the citizens of France, though you are an Englishman."

Ezra suppressed a smile. As far as he could remember, it was the first time in his life he had been called an Englishman. "It would be an honour, sir."

"Be ready in half an hour," said Dumas. "We will find you a horse. I am taking a patrol out; it will not matter if we make a detour. We will put you on the road to Valenciennes, and from there the diligence to Paris will be a matter of days, two if you are lucky. There you can do the American Regiment a favour."

"Lieutenant Colonel Dumas, I am most grateful."

"I would have been glad to keep you here – and so, no doubt, would the general. But you have more than done your duty to France tonight. The English have few friends in Paris, so you would do well to conceal your nationality – but as you were born, like me, in the Caribbean, perhaps the truth will be your best defence."

Half an hour later Ezra had bundled up his equipment and stood waiting as two soldiers rounded the barn mounted on a pair of bays, hard-working animals but with bright eyes and the look of horses used to speed and war. In between them they led a strange-looking yellow farm horse, its legs as unusually short as its body was unusually long. Ezra sighed. He would have to take whatever he could get. At least, he thought to himself, he would be closer to the ground if he should have cause to fall. The soldiers, Jérémie and Carter, could not help laughing as Ezra mounted the farm animal.

Carter was one of the actual Americans, his voice pitched far across the other side of the Atlantic, although he spoke in French like the rest.

"You look a picture, doctor, if you don't mind me saying."

Ezra shook his head, smiling, patting the yellow horse's neck. "Better than no horse at all," he said. He knew it was all they could spare.

It was still early and it was very cold. The line of horses snaked out along a farm track, their breath hanging in the air and their hooves thudding dully through the heavy mud. Ezra had never seen a battlefield, and he had always imagined two great shining armies, all dressed in bright colours, banners flying, facing each other across a field. At a trumpet blast, they would career towards each other, yelling perhaps, he had not thought in too much detail.

He could already tell this would not be anything like that.

Through a line of ruined trees he could see a few twists of smoke, the fires of the enemy. The men at the front of the line were quiet, wary. There could be snipers hiding anywhere. The fear was infectious. The horses passed alongside a field of winter rye, and suddenly there was a roar, a chorus of yelling and a volley of small arms.

The yellow horse catapulted forward and Ezra hung on to its mane for dear life.

The field was alive with the enemy. They must have been hiding there, waiting for them! Ezra's heart was suddenly in his mouth – the regiment would be set upon, and Loveday would never know what had happened to him. He cursed – he was a fool to think only of himself at such a time. The stumpy farm horse kept going, hell for leather, for a clump of trees out of the fighting. Ezra turned back and saw Dumas gallop into the rye, calling to his men, waving his sword and disarming a rifleman in an instant. What was almost as terrible as the cries of the men were the screams of the horses, almost unearthly. It was like watching hell, Ezra thought. The fourteen men of the American Regiment were hopelessly outnumbered. The enemy was everywhere – mostly Dutch, wearing the coloured coats of the Hapsburg emperor, one of the many enemies of the French revolution who thought that now might be a good time to invade and restore the French king. But Lieutenant Colonel Dumas, nearly a foot taller than anyone on the field and majestic on his black horse, cut them down like stalks of wheat.

The farm horse came to a stop, and Ezra felt the sweat cool on his brow. Dumas's men would be overcome, he should ride back to camp and fetch reinforcements. He kicked the horse on – it stayed put. He grunted in frustration and tried again, but still it would not move one inch. Ezra looked on helplessly as the field became a mass of noise and of gunshot so loud he imagined his head would explode.

There at the centre of the fighting was Dumas, his

horse rearing and pitching in the half-grown rye. Ezra watched, frozen, as an enemy soldier stood up barely inches from the lieutenant colonel, gun in hand. The world slowed – Ezra heard himself shouting, a strangled "Look out!", but Dumas didn't hear; they were too far away. His flashing blade was no match, surely, for a gun? The man was doomed.

Ezra heard the shot, one among many – and he saw Dumas in that same instant bring his blade down and deflect the bullet. Dumas's horse turned. The man with the gun was felled; there was an arc of blood spurting up into the air – Ezra recognized the result of a neatly severed jugular.

Hands trembling, Ezra slid down from his farm horse. There would be men down there who needed his help. He could not sit and watch; he had to do something.

By the time he reached the field the fighting was all but over, the enemy for the most part either fallen or fled or taken prisoner. Ezra set to work, dressing the wounds of Carter, who had suffered a gunshot to the thigh. The men were weary but in high spirits – except for the Dutch prisoners of war, who sat on the ground, hands on heads, while Jérémie relieved them of their weapons and Lieutenant Colonel Dumas regarded them, imperious, from his horse.

He addressed them in French, and then, when they remained unmoved, perfect Dutch.

Ezra was fluent in French, but his Dutch was less polished – all the same, he could just about follow. "Gentlemen," Dumas said, "you have been captured by the American Regiment of the French Revolutionary Army."

There were some murmurs of "Devils!" but Jérémie fixed the offenders with a scowl as he gathered up their guns and swords.

"We will treat you well, you have my word. We fight hard, because we fight for our country and ourselves, our families and loved ones. This is our land – it belongs to all of us. We will not give way. We are not serfs; we no longer serve the capricious kings and emperors who think of their subjects as no more than pawns on some chess-board. We fight for the simple reason that we are equal. All of us citizens in this new country!"

Dumas spoke plainly, yet there was so much pride in the man that Ezra could not help feeling his own heart swell. Surely there could be no better battle than this? The men of the American Regiment cheered. The Dutch soldiers remained sullen.

Carter looked poorly; Ezra doused his wound with a small amount of spirit and instructed the man to bite down hard on a rag. The ball was buried deep in his muscle, but thankfully had missed the bone.

Ezra's knife worked fast – a wound on the thigh might look insignificant, but he had seen men die from a nicked femoral artery there.

Carter's face screwed up in pain as the knife worked through his flesh. The ball was deeper than Ezra had thought. He reached for a scalpel; he needed something small and sharp. If he severed too much muscle the man's leg would take for ever to heal. Ezra found the ball, pulled it out and, as fast as he could manage, sewed up the thigh with small neat stitches, taking care not to pull the skin too tight, nor to leave the wound uncovered. There. He studied the result; not bad at all.

"You, doctor," Carter said, his face pale, "are a blessing; an angel of sorts."

Lieutenant Colonel Dumas rode over. "Master Sawbones, truly we should not let you go!" For a moment Ezra was worried he might really mean it – but Dumas was smiling. "You have served the Revolutionary Army well. Go, but deliver that letter, and as soon as you can."

Jérémie dumped an armful of the enemy's weapons on the ground. "Take one of these – go on, Monsieur Surgeon, you have earnt it."

Ezra knew little of guns or swords. "I cannot," he protested.

"Jérémie is right," Dumas said, "there will be those who would make trouble. Whatever the revolution says about us being brothers, there are plenty who do not believe it. Especially as you are English! Take a short sword – the Spanish steel – and a pistol, a small one. Carter will show you its use, but then I'm afraid we must leave you. You will have to make for Valenciennes alone; we must take the prisoners back to the general."

Jérémie handed Ezra a pistol, almost new, polished wood with a darker handle and brass on the barrel. It felt heavy in his hand, and was still warm from being fired. The cause of more death and injury and pain. Ezra was not squeamish – he spent his days cutting up human flesh and examining cadavers – but all the work he did was to protect life. A scalpel was very different from a sword. And as for a pistol…

Ezra's unease must have showed on his face, because Lieutenant Colonel Dumas looked hard at him. "You may be a surgeon, a good one, and from what I have seen a good man. But the revolution is not a seamstresses' tea party. Take it. If not for you then to protect your friends, the ones you seek."

Dumas was right. "Yes, sir," said Ezra, putting the pistol away.

"Ride west. You will reach the road before long, there will be a sign to town. And have no fear for the enemy. These Hapsburgs were way off course, and you're a single traveller on, if I may say, a very unthreatening mount. Keep your head down, young Ezra, and be willing to help the revolution – and if not God, then France and her citizens will help you en route."

He leant down and shook Ezra's hand.

"Your grip is a steady one, sir," Ezra said. "You would make a good surgeon yourself, I have no doubt. I thank you and your men for your hospitality."

"It is my men who should thank you. We owe you. Every man. You saved more than a few lives, and if there is any favour I can ever do you in return, just ask." Colonel Dumas smiled. "Now, go. Give that horse of yours a good kick and he will fly all the way to Valenciennes!"

The whole platoon laughed their goodbyes. That yellow horse would take its own sweet time.

Ezra walked back up the slope to where the farm horse stood searching out the last frozen spikes of grass among the fallen, rotten leaves. Ezra picked up the reins and swung into the saddle. Down below, the platoon were heading back to camp, their prisoners strung out behind them in a line.

Ezra felt the weight of the pistol tucked into his

jacket, thumping against his ribs, cushioned only by the crisp and newly printed French assignats – bank notes he had bought in London – that Mrs Boscaven had insisted on sewing into his clothes. The gun felt dangerous and it was not even loaded any longer. Still, he imagined Loveday would be singularly impressed, and perhaps it would turn out to be of use.

He pulled the horse's head up and headed away from the sunrise, into the mist and the damp of a French spring.

Chapter Two

The Diligence Between Valenciennes and Paris
20 March 1793

The diligence bounced and rocked, the four horses taking the road at great speed, hurtling towards Paris as fast as sinew and hoof allowed. Ezra had been warned about making this journey, first by the English newspapers and his friends back in London, and then by the boatmen in Dover – told over and over again that he was a fool to set out for Paris given that the French king had been guillotined and the old order overturned in favour of revolutionary chaos.

But Paris was not a battlefield, and there had been many besides himself waiting at Valenciennes for a place in the carriage.

With every rut and furrow Ezra felt the hard shape of the gun against his body, reminding him, as if it were necessary, of the battle he had witnessed; the shouting and the carnage he had seen in the rye field.

Surely someone like himself, someone so attuned to the nature of death, should take such things in his stride? Instead, the awful picture seemed seared into his brain. He longed for the peace and certainty of his laboratory in

London, the order of the operating theatre – a world in which he was in control.

Sleep came fitfully as the carriage leapt and swayed. He found himself dreaming of Loveday, rightly furious that he was late, producing Mahmoud, safe and sound, from where she'd found him under the floorboards in their Parisian boarding house. Then she made supper for the three of them, some kind of cheese, hot and melted— He woke up, jolted suddenly against a fellow passenger – a farmer's wife who was making the journey with her son. Ezra apologized and realized that the smell from his dream was in fact real; the pair were weighed down with what smelt like the entire cheese produce of the Ardennes.

Apart from the cheesemongers, the travellers were all asleep. These included an elderly man, worried he hadn't heard from his son since harvest, and a youth off to a new apprenticeship with a saddler in Saint Laurent. The youth, he could not be more than thirteen, was now dozing, mouth wide open, dribbling onto his chest. Ezra was glad he was asleep. The boy was harmless enough, but that first evening at the coaching inn in Valenciennes he had followed Ezra around like a puppy, eyes wide. He'd never seen a real-life "American", and could not stop himself from reaching out and touching Ezra's skin, his hair.

Ezra supposed it would be the same outside of any big city: the looks, the stares. His brief stay with the American Regiment had been the first time he'd been with so many people who looked like him. There were others with dark skin in London, of course; there were the famous black dances, he had heard of them. But the master had never been one to encourage dancing, and Ezra had not felt the need to do so himself. The more he thought about it, the more he felt that his skin had only ever really been a small disadvantage when men were drunk or ignorant, and if it wasn't for the happy accident of Mr McAdam, renowned as the foremost surgeon in the entire world, arriving on the island of Jamaica in time for his sale, then his future could have been very different.

Ezra had had the dual misfortune of having been born to a slave and with a tremendous tumour on his face. The master, travelling the Caribbean, had seen a small boy, head weighed down by the massive growth, and offered to remove it and take it back to London to study the thing. To do so, of course, he had had to buy Ezra, the boy who came with the tumour, and he had lived with Mr McAdam from that time. The surgeon had seen to it that he received a good education, and had eventually taken him on as an apprentice.

As Ezra sat in the diligence, he traced the scar on his face and gave thanks he had not ended up dead on a plantation – or, perhaps worse, alive in some freak show.

Outside, beyond the leather flap that covered the window, morning was breaking. Ezra could see the cool early morning light squeeze into the airless carriage and hear the odd snatch of birdsong as the diligence thundered through countryside towards the city.

Ezra had a mission – to meet Loveday and help her find Mahmoud, then to deliver Lieutenant Colonel Dumas's letter. He also planned to visit the largest hospital in Paris, the Hôtel-Dieu, to see the young surgeons he'd met at Mr McAdam's funeral. They'd told him then about the experiments into prolonging human life they'd been carrying out, and they'd invited him to visit them and see for himself. At the time he could have imagined nothing more exciting, but now he could barely remember that feeling. It seemed like an afterthought – all he wanted was to know that Loveday and Mahmoud were both safe and well.

He told himself for what must have been the hundredth time that there would surely be nothing to worry about. Loveday was the most capable girl he had ever met, even if she could be hot-headed. Mahmoud could be a little too imperious for his own good, but he was not stupid. And if Loveday was cross that Ezra had taken so long to arrive, she would forgive him soon – especially when he presented her with the fine pistol tucked inside his coat. They would surely find Mahmoud without incident – if, indeed, Loveday had not found him already – and then Ezra would deliver Lieutenant Colonel Dumas's letter. Once the Ottoman prince had been set back on his course, Ezra would be able to spend a little while seeing what the French surgeons had to offer. Perhaps a week, or two at most, he thought to himself, and then a return to London and to regularity, to English voices and English food...

A few hours later the carriage clattered through the Porte Saint-Martin. Ezra tried to look out of the window – he wanted to see the city and get a measure of it; Loveday had told him of the beautiful palaces, the well-proportioned squares – but the cheesemonger shouted at him as soon as he opened it.

"*Sacré bleu!* We shall freeze!"

Ezra quietly closed the window and reminded himself again of Loveday's address. She had written that she was staying with theatricals – friends of her late father's, the Franconis, brother and sister – on a street called La Rue des Enfants Rouges. A strange name – red children – but maybe it was after a school, like the Bluecoats in London. He wished that one of his fellow travellers had been a Parisian: he asked them if they knew the area anyway, but they had as little idea as he did.

When the diligence finally came to a halt in the Place de Grève he was glad to feel firm cobbles under his feet and smell the familiar city fog of old clothes and woodsmoke, although it was overlaid by a stench that the other travellers assured Ezra was merely the tanneries and abattoirs that were situated in this quarter. The River Seine bordered the Place, and across the water stood the massive cathedral of Notre-Dame. If he hadn't been so used to great buildings – he was thinking of St Paul's, modern and quite perfect in every way – he might have gasped, but he was a Londoner, and quite accustomed, he told himself, to the marvel of capital cities. Across the bridges on the island in the Seine – the Île de la Cité – stood the very oldest parts of the city: the cathedral, the hospital, the Hôtel-Dieu, grey with the dirt of ages. Where were the boulevards, the squares and public gardens Loveday had told him about? He'd been expecting to be met with grandeur straight off the coach, but instead he seemed to have been set down in the middle of a filthy working city.

The driver and his boy brought down Ezra's luggage, a bag, not so heavy as to be a burden, containing only a set of clothes and his surgeon's instruments. The sword that Lieutenant Colonel Dumas had given him hung rather too showily at his waist and Ezra attempted to tuck it into his belt, but he was not used to the thing at all. In no time a gaggle of street boys had crowded around him and offered to point him in the right direction in exchange for a few *sous*.

"Hey, *Américain*!" they shouted in broken English. One of the smaller boys noticed his sword. "Are you a duellist? Hey, hey! *En garde!*"

"Monsieur American, you have money? Sugar? Bread?"

Ezra eyed them warily. "Rue des Enfants Rouges?" He held out a coin. The boys began an argument in their native tongue. Ezra tried to follow it – one boy insisted that was the street that used to be called, until last year at least, Rue des Hommes Armés. Several others were equally adamant it was now the Rue des Droits des Hommes, others still that it was near Les Halles.

"Yes!" Ezra seized on a place name he recognized. "The markets!"

There was more arguing among the boys, and Ezra noticed how thin they all were, and that their feet were wrapped in rags, or, if they were lucky, wooden clogs that looked far too big. His heart sank – surely the revolution ought to be providing for such people?

"I know it, citizen sir! It's where I was born and bred," one boy yelled. Behind him a smaller boy, with dirty blond hair and a ruddy complexion, elbowed his way into the scrum.

"He weren't so much bred, sir," the small boy said, also in French, "as dragged up by wolves. Tame ones, though – ones who taught him how to lay a table and talk nice."

The bigger boy rolled his eyes. "Pay Luc no attention – he will turn everything into nonsense. He wasn't even born in the city!"

"But I know it now, *monsieur*!" insisted the smaller boy.

Ezra smiled and found another coin, then promised them one each. The boy called Luc grinned; Jean, the bigger boy, leant close.

"I am the oldest! If you give me his coin I will look after it for him. He'll only spend it on buns."

Luc was indignant. "If there *are* any buns! There are never buns these days."

Ezra bent down and spoke to the pair of them in his best French. He hoped it was good enough. "My friends, surely, as citizens of Paris, you deserve equal pay? Is that not what your revolution is about?" The boys goggled at him, and then began an argument too thick with slang for Ezra to follow.

"Well," Ezra went on, "it is cold, and if you are too busy arguing, I will find another to conduct me—"

The boys stopped immediately. The smaller one jerked his head and Ezra followed the pair out of the Place and away from the river along a tiny cobbled street where the buildings jutted so far out over his head they almost blocked out the light. Ezra supposed that Loveday must still have plenty of money from the sale of the sultan's ruby – getting a good price for it had been the only reason she and Mahmoud had stopped in Paris in the first place, and they would have travelled onwards by now if Mahmoud had not disappeared. Surely, he hoped, she could afford some decent rooms.

As they left the riverside, Ezra noticed a tannery taking up an entire block. Armies of people were hard at work, crouching over processing pits filled with foul-smelling lye and urine as children scurried to and fro, carrying bundles on their heads. All the workers wore rags wrapped round their faces to keep out the stench.

The boys ahead sped up as they passed into a street of butchers; in every open courtyard, every space, was some animal, tethered, lowing its last. The air was thick with the smell of blood, rivulets of it flowing down into the gutter in the centre of the street. Ezra reminded himself he had seen worse in Smithfield.

They came upon a small crowd blocking the street, all shouting and cheering and betting, in French and in other languages Ezra didn't know. Ezra recognized this as bull-baiting – one sad black bull, eyes dulled, was surrounded by at least two dogs, snapping and barking at it. One of the dogs' jowls were red with blood where it had already torn the bull's throat. The bull staggered, the dogs wagged their tails – it would be over soon. Cities, Ezra thought, were much the same everywhere.

The houses were old here, and tall, leaning out over streets that were only just wide enough for a man leading a skinny donkey. As they walked, though, the streets began to widen, the houses became more modern. The older boy, Jean, must have noticed Ezra taking it all in.

"Loads of the nobs have gone and left," he said.

"All of them?" Ezra asked.

"No, there's still plenty of money around," said Luc. "Merchants, and that. I wanted to be an apprentice but *mon vieux* didn't have the money. He just packed me off to the north and bade me seek my fortune."

"There was no father, I bet," Jean sneered. "I reckon you never had one. I bet your mother—"

"Don't you dare insult *ma mère*. I swear I will knock you down. She was a pearl, a queen."

Jean smirked. "So why ain't you there looking after her? Why don't you go back to where you came from and leave Paris to us *Parisiens*?"

"Isn't Paris for everyone?" Ezra asked, attempting to diffuse the argument he could see about to break out.

"Not for the likes of him, that sheep's son from Gascony!" Jean spat and Luc turned on him.

"Why, you dog!" Luc yelled. "You'll not insult my mother, you son of a turd!"

Ezra stepped between them, but Luc ducked around him and kicked at Jean. Jean went to cuff Luc, but he just slapped him away with a laugh and Jean let off a volley of expletives and oaths. Ezra could not understand most of them, but the words were loosed with such venom and spit that he felt enough of the meaning was clear.

"Stop it! Both of you." Ezra held the two boys apart. "I do not care for your squabbles. I merely want directions. I shall walk away from you both without paying you." He glared at one and then the other. "Now, shake hands," Ezra said. "At least pretend that you are gentlemen."

"We are not gentlemen, American," Luc said. "Although I can tell you a good joke about an American and a—"

"Not again!" Jean protested. "I have heard that a dozen times. I will not go one step further with you, you turnip-brained, cheating southerner."

"Leave him, American. I can show you the way. Jean is not as bad as he pretends. He has no mother at all so he throws mud at mine. Have you heard the one about the mutton-headed Parisian?" Luc shouted after his friend.

Jean, who had already made it to the end of the street, turned and made a gesture of the lowest sort. Ezra raised an eyebrow.

"He is angry with me because I beat him at dominoes. He will be my friend again tomorrow." Luc shrugged. "We and all the boys who sleep in the empty buildings between Les Halles and Le Marais have a motto: *All for one and one for all*." He led Ezra around a corner. "Come along, American – we are nearly there."

There was a strong odour of burning as Luc led Ezra through a series of covered alleys into a small narrow street. Ezra wrinkled his nose. It was more than smoke from chimneys. Something big had burned; the smell hung in the air.

"We are here, *monsieur*." Luc held out a grubby hand, and Ezra fished in his pocket for the coins.

Something seemed wrong about this street. It was strangely light, that was it. He looked up – and saw why. All of the buildings on the north side were in ruins, still smoking, burned so badly that only the odd finger of timber, a fire-blackened charcoal claw, stood up against a yawning space of pale grey sky.

Luc saw him looking. "Ah yes." He pocketed the coins. "The fire, day before yesterday and the ruin still smoking. That baker was a good one, and his wife always gave us the stale loaves. The tailor's next door burned down too, and the glove-maker's, and the house where the acrobats lived – from the circus over on the Rue Saint-Honoré. Five houses gone, burned to nothing before they could put it out. Jean swears it was spies, but I heard it was a lamp turned over in the night."

Ezra wasn't listening. He looked from one side of the street to the other, then took out the address – this had to be the place – the acrobats, that was it. What had Loveday said, she was staying with a brother and sister, performers? It was them, he was certain. He felt his insides twist and sink; for a moment he was frozen where he stood, then he gave a cry and dashed hell for leather into the nearest ruin, ignoring Luc's protests behind him. He was about to push through the blackened doorframe when he felt a hand on his shoulder pulling him away. He wheeled round to see an old man with a broom – he'd been sweeping the front of a shop on the other side of the street.

"Whoa, citizen, don't go in there, it's dangerous."

Ezra almost replied in English. "My friend, she was living here. I must find her!"

"All gone now, and nobody there, either. Two nights they burned. My bricks were hot to touch, I nearly sent my wife out to stay with her mother."

Ezra took deep breaths. The place was a shell. He could see there was no point in looking through those ashes for anything, let alone anyone.

He swallowed. "What happened?"

"We were lucky not to catch it this side of the street," the man said. "The whole row went up like fireworks – in fact that's what the most of us thought it was. Then the roofs fell in and they all ran out screaming like a pack of rats. Poor souls."

"Were there any fatalities?" said Ezra, desperate.

"Calm down, citizen. *Des morts?* What's that accent? American, is it?"

The shopkeeper looked at Luc, who was still hanging around. "Is he from the colonies?"

Luc shrugged. The shopkeeper spoke slowly as if he thought Ezra was an idiot.

"There were nine dead including Georges and his family – his wife, Jeanne…"

"What about the acrobats? The circus people?"

"At the end of the street? Just some kids – three, I think – since the old man snuffed it. Snappy dressers they were." He paused.

Ezra looked at him. "What about a girl, red-haired, Mademoiselle Finch?"

The shopkeeper frowned. "*La fille anglaise?* Ah, she pretended she was not!" He shrugged. "Her accent was not bad. But she was so loud. You know what they are like – I should have called the guard to lock her up. Enemies of the revolution, every one of them. *Les anglais!*" He said it like a curse and spat on the ground. "It would not surprise me if that girl was a spy."

Ezra covered his shock. "Have you seen her? Since the fire? Any of them?"

"Come to think of it…" The man frowned thought-fully. Ezra willed him to say something good. She couldn't be dead. Loveday could not die.

The man shook his head. "It would not surprise me if she had started the fire herself. I know those English dogs want to see us suffer! It is good for her that she is dead."

Ezra pressed his hand against his eyes. He had not for one second imagined that he would travel all this way only to find she was not here.

"I think the bodies went to the hospital – well, what was left of the poor devils. Although that one deserved all she got. You could go and look, though I don't know if you'd be able to tell one from the other."

"The Hôtel-Dieu? They're there?"

"That's the one. You wouldn't catch me going – I saw some of the things they brought out." He made a face. "Burnt to a crisp, and the smell!"

Ezra took another deep breath. He had to steady himself. He had to think.

"Some people came out alive. They must have done. You're *sure* you haven't seen Mademoiselle Finch?"

"I said, didn't I?" The Frenchman rolled his eyes at Luc. "Foreigners."

"I am a surgeon. Mademoiselle Finch is a good person. She is…" He stopped himself.

"You know her, *hein*?" The shopkeeper smiled; his teeth were only marginally less blackened than the ruined terrace. "Well, you might be the National Convention for all I know, but there's no way any of those bodies is getting any better, whoever you are!"

Ezra turned suddenly to Luc. "A whole franc if you show me the way to the hospital."

"Hôtel-Dieu? Everyone knows that place." Luc set off, and Ezra bid the shopkeeper goodbye then hurried after the boy, his mind turning over and over. Loveday

34

could be dead – but no, he needed proof. He was a man of science. He would not think the worst, not yet.

Up ahead, the French boy almost disappeared out of sight and Ezra had to speed up so as not to lose him. He stumbled and had to right himself against a wall. He was out of breath and it felt like there was a lump in his throat the size of an apple. Ezra swallowed hard and wiped some city grit out of his eye. He had to get to the hospital as soon as possible. There he would see the bodies, and then he would know for certain what had happened to Loveday.

He tried not to think about what he might find.

Chapter Three

The Hôtel-Dieu
Île de la Cité
Paris
20 March 1793

Luc ran across the Pont Notre-Dame and Ezra followed. He could see that half of the houses had been cleared away from one side of the bridge – the builders were making a mess of removing the houses on the other, narrowing the roadway in the process, which meant Ezra had to dodge all manner of pedlars and street sellers. As they approached the far side Ezra could now see the grey, grimy building at close quarters. Luc stopped at a set of gates, heavy and wooden, with a smaller door set into one side. The hospital looked just as old as the cathedral of Notre-Dame, its close neighbour.

"I'm not going in there. It's full of sick people." He leant close. "Don't know what you might catch. Go in with a blister or a pimple, come out with some plague, then sicken and…" The boy mimed a knife across his throat and made a gargling sound. "I'll leave you here, American, if that suits you."

Ezra nodded. *Hôtel-Dieu*, the sign read, *AD 651*. The

place was even older than St Bartholomew's back home in London.

Luc tugged at his sleeve. "A coin, citizen? You did promise."

"Yes, yes, I did. Here, take this." He handed over the coin and the boy's face lit up.

"You are too kind, Monsieur American."

Ezra knocked on the wooden door as Luc scurried away; it opened a minute later, and a man with a beard that reached all the way down to his chest looked out. "*Ouais?*" he said.

Ezra stood tall. "The bodies, from the fire at…" He looked for Luc but Luc had vanished back across the bridge. "At Rue des…" Ezra tried to remember. *Armed Men? Red children?* "Rue des Hommes Rouges!"

The gatekeeper laughed. "Look, citizen." He sucked on a long clay pipe. "Whoever you are, this is a hospital." He spoke to Ezra as if he was a very small child. "You may be from America. You may be the richest sugar baron in all of France, I do not care. We are not letting any visitors in."

He went to close the door but Ezra stopped it with his foot.

"Wait! I am a friend of Monsieur Bichat. I am a surgeon." He bit his tongue to stop himself from adding where exactly he had met the French surgeon. Being "American" may well work in his favour, but being from London might not. "Monsieur Bichat and Monsieur Figaud! They know me. They invited me to meet the director Monsieur Desault. Please! I beg you."

The gatekeeper looked Ezra up and down. Time seemed to slow. A cart approached and the man had to open the whole gate, which he did at a pace that would have shamed a snail. If he had been Loveday, Ezra thought, he would have dashed straight in, through what looked like a medieval courtyard and into the massive stone building on the other side. But he was not.

Instead, he opened his bag and took out his instrument case.

"Look. These are my surgical instruments. See?" He said the words slowly, in French, and loudly. "I am a surgeon."

The gatekeeper spat into the gutter. "*Je ne comprends pas.*"

"You don't understand?"

Ezra thought hard. Perhaps he was telling the man he was a musician rather than a surgeon. Perhaps his accent was off. Ezra took out the bone saw and mimed cutting. The man stepped back.

"Surgeon?" Ezra said. "Cutting? See?"

The cart rolled inside. The gatekeeper looked at Ezra. He tipped the contents of his pipe out against the wall, snorted, then spat again. Then, still painfully slowly, he began to close the gate.

"Please? Sir?"

The man stopped. He gave Ezra a filthy look. "American," he said, the gate still half open. "We are all citizens here. You would do well to remember that."

"Yes, of course." Ezra paused, corrected himself. "Citizen."

The gatekeeper nodded. "Citizen Bichat is very busy. He may see you. He may not. And I will take a coin for my trouble."

Ezra felt a wash of relief. He stepped inside and heard the thud as the heavy wooden gates shut behind him. He gave the man a coin and asked for the mortuary. It was in the least lovely building, set hard against the river – as it ought to have been, Ezra thought. He knew hospitals, he knew mortuaries; they were always in the coolest, quietest spaces, away from the wards and living patients.

Ezra nodded, thanked the man, then gathered himself and set off. He would find Messieurs – no, *Citizens* – Bichat and Figaud later.

"Hey!" the gatekeeper called. "Hey! I said I will send a boy to take you!"

Ezra didn't wait. He made straight for the mortuary.

He could smell them first. That high, sweet, burnt smell, like the winter hog roasts of Christmas fairs. But this was not hog. He took the stone steps down and knocked at the door, addressed the young man with the running nose who answered it and was led into a low cellar. Ezra could hear the slap of water from the river, just on the other side of the wall, and feel the damp. This youth seemed not to care whether the visitor was a surgeon or not; he just held out his hand for what he termed "viewing money" and let Ezra in.

"I don't know what they want with these," he said with an indifferent shrug. "I mean, it's not as if you can dissect them, they're too far gone."

There were four skulls, blackened in parts and red-roasted in others. Ezra reminded himself he had seen such things before, if not many times then more than once. And wasn't drowning worse, when the flesh was swollen and putrid, rather than griddled?

He was a professional.

It was hard to tell age, sex, anything, but he did his best. The teeth of one skull were ruined, another had a pierced ear – no doubt an earring had been slipped off by the boy with the running nose, or whoever had brought the bodies here. Loveday did not have pierced ears.

One skull was considerably smaller than the others, a young child, flesh burned off to reveal bone. That just left the one. There was no hair, and the face, what was left of it, was quite cooked, the eyeballs melted, the lips drawn back in a permanent grimace. Could it be her? His legs felt weak.

Ezra steeled himself. He must do this. He picked up the fourth skull again, but there was no way in heaven he could tell who this poor soul had once been. As he turned it over a tooth was dislodged and fell. He bent down to the floor and picked it up, turning it over in his hand. It was yellowed, old; Loveday was only fifteen, and he knew her teeth were whiter than this. It was not her. Ezra had to steady himself against the table in his relief. There was no saying where she might be, dead or alive. But she was not lying here in this mortuary.

There was a noise on the steps behind him and he heard the running-nose boy sniff and apologize, and then there were footsteps, hard leather boots on the stone flags.

"Ezra McAdam!" The sound bounced off the roof and Ezra put the skull down with a start. "Ezra McAdam, what brings you down here? We had your letter from London; we were expecting you days ago. The revolution needs to make its mark on our woeful transport!

I am so pleased to see you here, safe and sound!"

Ezra quickly wiped his eyes on his sleeve and blinked hard. He composed himself a little and turned around. "Monsieur Bichat! Yes, I am arrived at last."

The French surgeon was smiling broadly, and despite their surroundings, despite everything, Ezra found his spirits lift at the sight of a familiar face. The man passed Ezra a cloth to wipe his hands, and then shook Ezra's firmly and warmly.

"I am so glad you are here! I must admit I was quite worried, I thought perhaps this might not be the best time to travel. I imagine it can't have been easy to find a crossing?"

"No, sir. I had to beg a place on a fishing boat – well, they said they were fishermen."

"Smugglers?"

Ezra nodded.

Bichat frowned. "The whole world stands against the new republic, and honest travellers – and trade – are suffering."

"Yes, I ran into the war in the north on my way here. Some of the regiments are in need of a good surgeon – well, any surgeon. But as I said in my letter, I have come to find some friends. One has gone missing, a young boy, and another … well… That is why I was down here. I thought she might have … the fire." He turned away again, looked at the remains, sticks of charcoal and sinew. "I have examined the bodies and I do not believe any of these to be her, but I have no idea where she might be. She is English, and I fear for her safety."

Bichat looked at Ezra, not without sympathy. "Paris

is a large city, *mon ami*. You have searched for her in only one place. And if she has committed no crime against the republic, I am sure she must have nothing to fear."

Ezra nodded. He didn't tell Bichat that Loveday had been escorting Ottoman royalty to Constantinople, and that he doubted the republic would look on that kindly. Loveday would have the sense not to tell anyone that, wouldn't she? Perhaps the French surgeon was right.

"Come," said Bichat gently, "you are quite chilled. I still have some brandy, and it is very, very good."

Ezra allowed Bichat to steer him out of the mortuary and across the gardens. They were beautiful, but of another, earlier time, low shrubs of box and rosemary trimmed hard into shapes interspersed with new spring flowers, yellow primroses and crocuses, in among stone colonnades like a monastery or a palace. It was calm and quiet, a refreshing change from the filthy chaos of the city outside, but Ezra was still worrying about Loveday.

Bichat waved a hand around. "There were old buildings here that burned down years ago. We are hoping the revolution will mean we can build again. In stone, for the future." Ezra hadn't heard him. "We will be able to treat the whole city. New wards, new ideas!"

Ezra nodded as Bichat went on about all the opportunities afforded by the revolution, which he admitted brought some difficulties but was on the whole a very good thing.

"Especially for men of science, like ourselves."

Suddenly the calm was split in two as a bell in the cathedral next door shattered the serenity of the hospital garden.

Bichat saw Ezra jump and laughed. "That is the only bell left, the one that strikes the hour. They have melted the rest of them down for cannons. Oh, you should have heard them before, when they rang for weddings or for saints' days or holidays. We used to say those bells were loud enough to raise the dead from slumber!" He gave Ezra a look. "But we have found something else that works a little better."

Ezra sat down in the surgeon's office. It was plain and austere, rows of jars containing fingers and toes, a patella and a hip joint; on the walls medical prints and certificates and honours awarded to Monsieur Bichat and the hospital. Ezra began to feel more at home. He tried to remind himself what Mr McAdam would do, he would never have given in to emotion. There was nothing Ezra could do for Loveday at this moment – he ought, at least, to take this opportunity to learn from his fellow surgeons while he was here.

Bichat poured out two glasses of golden liquid. Ezra wasn't one for strong drink, but he took the glass and sipped at it, and found that it restored him a little.

"You must be exhausted," his friend commented. "If you don't mind me saying, you look ready to drop. My home is not far, just across the river, but tonight I will find a room for you here in the hospital. Our director, Citizen Desault, is out of town at present, but tomorrow Citizen Figaud will be here – and you will meet Citizen Desault's newest protégé, Samuel Renaud. He is, I think, only a year or so older than yourself; he trained in northern Italy with Galvani, and he has incredible ideas!"

As darkness began to fall, Bichat led Ezra across the main courtyard towards the wing furthest from the entrance, and up a staircase that to Ezra seemed interminable. The room at the top was sparse but adequate, with a small window and plain white walls.

Ezra imagined he would have trouble sleeping; that thoughts of Loveday and the fire might keep him awake. But his body was so relieved to find a proper bed, with sheets and blankets and a fine warm coverlet, that his eyes closed, and before he could begin to make plans he slipped easily into a dreamless sleep.

He woke with the sound of the single bell of Notre-Dame, and counted the hour for five o'clock. It was dark still, and his breath made clouds of condensation even though the grate showed the remains of a recent fire.

Fire.

He turned over and shut his eyes. He must concentrate now on finding Mahmoud. But how could he do that without talking to Loveday, without knowing what the two of them had been doing before the prince disappeared? He opened his eyes again and stared up at the ceiling. In one corner a web had caught the dust, the work of one tiny spider. In the dim light Ezra found himself studying it, mesmerized by the intricate structure.

If a creature of no importance or worth had managed such a feat, then surely he might somehow, some way, find one young prince in a city full of people.

He would retrace their steps. He would find out where they had been when they were still together, and where Loveday had searched after Mahmoud had disappeared. Perhaps the Russians had found him first – in which case

Ezra should not discount the possibility that Mahmoud may be dead by now.

He swallowed, sat up. He must set to work. Make notes, make some kind of structure out of the chaos all around.

Ezra dressed and got out his notebook. There was a small wooden table in the room; he lit the candle stub and searched in his jacket for a pencil. As he did so, his hand settled on Lieutenant Colonel Dumas's letter. He took that out and placed it on the mantelpiece; he must not forget he'd made a promise to deliver it.

This morning he would talk to the shopkeeper in the Rue des Enfants Rouges. He would be calm and measured. He would find the boy, Luc, who'd helped him yesterday – maybe Mahmoud was living out on the streets as he'd done in London. All for one and one for all, hadn't Luc said? Maybe that would apply to Mahmoud as well.

He would take Dumas's letter, too. He looked at the address: the Place des Victoires. That should be easy enough to find.

It was perfectly light when Bichat called on him. He had brought a breakfast picnic his wife had made, wrapped up in a basket – and Monsieur Figaud was with him, the second French surgeon Ezra had met at his master's funeral. Figaud was the same age as Bichat, perhaps thirty at most, but his face was lined and Ezra swore he saw grey in his hair that hadn't been there last year in London. He seemed tired, as if a great weight had dropped upon him, but he was pleased to see Ezra.

"It is good to see you again, *mon ami*," he said, stooping

to heat the pot of coffee he'd brought with him on the fire. "Things in Paris, they have been difficult lately."

"But the advances we have been making," said Bichat, "have been astonishing. You must see them."

Bichat seemed keen to make sure their English guest did not feel his visit was wasted, and Ezra felt a little bad asking if he might leave the hospital tour for another day.

"I have business in the city. I should like to investigate my friend's disappearance," Ezra explained. He was wary of mentioning Mahmoud. "And the sooner I begin..."

Bichat wiped his mouth. "Ezra, I must warn you, it will not be good for you, an Englishman, to be turning over stones looking for answers to questions that do not need answering."

Figaud nodded wearily. "Bichat is right. Sleeping dogs must lie, as you say in English."

Ezra bit his lip. He was, after all, their guest.

"Has Bichat told you about our young prodigy, Renaud?" Figaud asked. "You absolutely must see his work – I believe he is close to your own age, it would be *splendide* for the two of you to meet."

"Yes, yes," said Bichat. "And we have something arranged for noon, and thought you would wish to accompany us."

Ezra reluctantly agreed. He could give them one day, at least; begin his investigations tomorrow. Perhaps touring the hospital would take his mind off his uncertainty over Loveday's fate.

The hospital smelt of filth and sickness, and Ezra had to try not to gag. Bichat apologized. The wards, he said, were in urgent need of modernization; patients were sometimes three or four to a bed.

"What are your infection levels, after operations?" Ezra asked.

Bichat frowned. "We try not to be invasive where we can help it. Wounds necrotize and fever is always higher once the weather gets warmer."

Figaud explained how they were hoping that once the country had stabilized, which he said was simply a matter of time, there would be new developments. "Of course, there has been some rebuilding already – our new laboratory is magnificent, the finest in France."

Bichat proudly agreed. "That is where we will find Citizen Renaud," he added. They crossed the gardens again; the laboratory was easy to spot, the brick building newer than most of those around it. As they approached, the doors swung open and a young man emerged. He was dressed like Bichat and Figaud in sombre, plain black, a jacket and trousers, and he, too, wore his hair cropped short and natural. Ezra could not help admiring these surgeons; they looked more modern than his colleagues in London, most of whom still wore ridiculous multi-coloured waistcoats and white curled wigs.

When the young man saw Ezra his face lit up.

"You must be Ezra McAdam? The young genius from London! Citizen Bichat told me yesterday that you had arrived – oh, I have so longed to meet you." Ezra could not help feeling flattered. "I am Samuel Renaud – come, come, I cannot wait to share my work."

Renaud was interrupted by the bell at Notre-Dame sounding for a quarter past eleven. Bichat looked unsure for a moment. "There is still a little time before the executions," he conceded.

"Executions?" asked Ezra, perplexed.

Renaud seemed to mistake his confusion for eagerness, because he waved a hand dismissively and led him in the direction of the laboratory. "You must see this first," he insisted.

Figaud smiled. "I will go ahead and secure us a cab. But our Renaud, he will not settle until he has shown you his work."

The French surgeons had been right – the laboratory was magnificent. It was fantastically appointed, tiled and equipped to a standard Ezra had not seen before. For a moment he forgot everything: Mahmoud, Loveday, the revolution. His mouth fell open as he took it all in: the high windows for light, the tables of wood and marble that ran the full length of both walls. He resolved to commit as many details to memory as he could. Maybe one day he would remodel the old laboratory in Great Windmill Street...

"Amazing, *non*?" Bichat said with a chuckle. "It turned out for the best when the School for Surgeons no longer wanted Renaud to carry out his work on their premises."

Ezra nodded dumbly. The tiling went from floor to ceiling; the floor was slightly angled, for drainage, and of marble too.

Instruments were stored in glass cupboards and on shelves that glittered in the spring sunshine. On one table was a kind of box holding four glass jars; all were partially filled with water, wired together and covered with what looked like copper foil. There was a black dial between the jars, and a set of strange copper balls suspended above them.

"Are those Leyden jars?" Ezra asked. He had read some papers about the storage of electricity.

"Yes, they are marvellous, are they not, and quite beautiful?" Renaud smiled eagerly. "It is my very own reworking of the electrostatic generator."

It felt, to Ezra, like nothing so much as stepping right into the future. He almost gasped aloud. "An influence machine!" Ezra had seen one at a lecture at the Royal Society in London. "Bichat said you studied with Galvani?"

"Yes! Before I took to surgery I was set to study the physical sciences," Renaud explained. "But that was before I realized the links between the physical and the electrical." Renaud turned to Ezra. "Did you know that all our muscles move by means of electrical impulses?"

Ezra nodded. "I know the theory, yes. I have seen the experiment, with frogs' legs rigged up to an influence machine like this one."

Then Ezra noticed something else. Upon the table-tops stood a series of bowls, each containing something about the size of a chicken plucked and ready to roast, and covered in a cloth. Ezra counted seven, three on one side, four on the other, Renaud stepped forward and whisked one of the cloths away.

Ezra gave a start.

A human head, severed high up the neck, lolled as if in waking sleep. Two grey eyes fixed on the lovely tiling, just as Ezra's had done. But these eyes were lifeless, the lips discoloured, and just below, where the neck had been neatly severed, the vertebra shone white in the mass of tubes and muscle.

Ezra had seen the heads of corpses, of course – although they were normally attached to their bodies. It was just surprising seeing one presented with the flourish a magician might use to produce a rabbit, that was all.

Renaud removed the other cloths one by one, and suddenly seven faces, seven surprised mouths and thirteen eyes were looking ceilingwards too, heads balanced in bowls. Hair shorn, men and women alike, their chins a variety of stubble and smooth – one, Ezra reckoned, was a year or two younger than himself.

"You are replicating Galvani's experiment on *humans*?"

Ezra could not disguise his distaste, and Renaud must have noticed.

There was a flash of irritation. "You think I use these corpses simply for amusement? This is not just mechanics, I assure you!"

"I am sure our English friend didn't mean..." began Bichat.

Ezra felt suddenly bold; why shouldn't he say exactly what he was thinking? "We may be surgeons, sir, but I believe we should afford the dead some respect. They were once as we are; they had children, fathers, mothers."

"Mr McAdam," said Bichat, holding up his hands with a laugh that seemed rather awkward to Ezra, "in life these were criminals – traitors to France, to the revolution."

"Even so," said Ezra, frowning, "this experiment has already been done. In fact I doubt there is a child in London who hasn't seen the frog's legs jump when a current is administered."

Renaud bristled. "You think me no better than a show-man? This is no trick or sideshow. It is not the electrical impulse that interests me, oh no, *citizen*!" He spat the word passionately. Ezra stepped back. "I am not interested in the flesh and blood, these bones, this human abattoir that has me sully my hands with the blood of criminals and wastrels! No. I am interested in what makes each of us above an animal, a sentient being, a human capable of thought and words." He lifted the head of an elderly man from its bowl and brought it close to the machine. "That part, the one religious fellows call the soul, resides alone in the head. Ancients used to believe the heart was the seat of our humanity. We know better, but I would know more still." He set the head down. "You have read the director's theories of vitalism?" Renaud began to crank the handle of the generator. "That life resides in both the organs and the brain? Well, I am on my way to redefine these theories. I believe all life can be found in the brain and the brain alone." Renaud cranked harder. "I must just build up the charge…"

Ezra looked at Bichat. This was something he had thought about himself, that the brain was more important than the heart – indeed, than any other organ.

"I understand we have much to learn about the brain." Ezra had to speak loudly over the hum of the generator.

Renaud grinned at him. "Exactly!"

The generator was louder now, the sound seemed to bounce around the walls, off the tiles and marble floor until the hum was practically unbearable. Bichat had covered his ears with his hands.

"Renaud has been doing marvellous work," he

shouted. "He is close to discovering the seat of life. To document the moment that spark of life leaves the body, and understand if it can exist alone, go on existing after the body has gone. It is truly astounding, is it not?"

Ezra watched the eager young surgeon take two filigree-thin copper wires and attach them to the old man's head: two to the temples, one either side, then another two where the main artery ran up to the brain.

He turned a dial. There was more noise.

"Watch!" Renaud indicated the head. "This is from two days past, another day more and the spark of life would be gone – look!"

Ezra did. He saw the eyelids flicker, once, twice; the eyeballs swivel to meet his, and for a second he was staring into the eyes of a man who was most certainly dead. The irises were black, the lens of the eyeball had not begun to come away. This is what he would have looked like in life. It was not a corpse, not a part of a corpse; this was a human being. Ezra felt the shock as real as a blow that had knocked the breath clean out of him. His own eyes goggled at this dead man who was seemingly alive.

The eyes fell shut. The power had been transmitted but the head remained … a head. Ezra realized he had staggered back, and he had to lean against the wall as he recovered himself.

"Consciousness!" Renaud shouted in triumph over the sound of the machine. "It is still there! All there!"

Ezra was still dazed as the noise of Renaud's machine finally died down. He told himself there should be no reason for the experiment to affect him. Hadn't he dissected, or assisted in more dissections, at least, than any anatomist in London? To be unsettled by this was hypocrisy – his knee-jerk response was as backwards, as foolish, as the voices of those who felt dissection was unnatural and reprehensible in spite of the advancements it brought. Science must move forward, and if Renaud truly could discover where life ended and death began, then wouldn't it be worthwhile? It was, as Renaud had said, truly groundbreaking.

"These were criminals, yes?" said Ezra, trying to sound – and to feel – less uneasy.

"Oh, yes," said Bichat. "There is an ample supply – there are so many executions, sometimes thirty come in the tumbrils from prisons all over the country in a single day."

"Every day?" Ezra could not hide his shock.

"It is unpleasant but true. This is a difficult time. There are enemies of the revolution everywhere." Bichat was serious.

"But in every cloud, I think you say in English, there is a silver lining." Renaud smiled. "The guillotine. It was my inspiration."

"How is that?"

"It was last summer. I had the good fortune to gain a seat so close to the stand that I could see every flicker, every nuance, of the victims' expressions." Renaud seemed a little too keen for Ezra's liking. "The execution is so swift and so precise, you see…"

"You will have a chance to witness it yourself this afternoon," put in Bichat. "We are viewing an execution at the Place de la Révolution, at noon. We ought to meet Citizen Figaud soon if we are to be on time."

Ezra had always done his best to avoid public

executions: the idea struck him as entirely inhumane. To his mind, as surgeons, their life's work was to restore health and life, not to extinguish it. But he walked with Renaud and Bichat past the old fellow on the gate to meet with Figaud, who had, true to his word, already hailed them a cab for the Place de la Révolution. As they climbed in, Ezra heard the driver say that it would be hard to get too close because of the crowd, even on a cold day like today.

Ezra knew about the guillotine, of course – had read about it in the papers – but he would have hoped that a revolution that could sweep away kings and lords might also do away with the institution of public murders. He looked at his fellow surgeons sitting with him in the cab, talking offhandedly as if they were all on a visit to the theatre.

A large lidded wicker basket sat between them on the floor of the carriage.

"To bring home the spoils!" Renaud grinned.

Chapter Four

The cab wove its way over the bridge and westwards. Up ahead, the imposing stone Hôtel de Ville, the town hall, was visible at a distance above the older wooden buildings. Ezra looked out across the river. It was busy with low flat barges, and he watched a few of them unloading barrels along the muddy riverside.

"You have more bridges than we do in London," Ezra said. "But I miss the high masted ships." In London the river felt like a city in itself, a mass of ships from all over the world. These barges, Bichat explained, travelled only from Rouen and Le Havre.

"The Seine is too shallow for ocean-going trade," he said. "Even when it rains."

Ezra nodded, but he found his mind pulled back to the event they were on their way to witness. "Do you attend the executions often?"

"Oh, yes," said Renaud. "You remember, Citizen Bichat, last summer, the day it rained tremendously?"

Bichat nodded.

"Well," Renaud went on animatedly, turning back to Ezra, "that day there were only five to meet Madame Guillotine, but one of them – the third – was exceptional. In life, no: a young woman, shorn hair, face that snarled rather than showed the usual feminine grace. But in death…"

Ezra said nothing, but he suspected it might be hard to show feminine grace if one's death was impending. He continued to hold his tongue as Renaud went on to describe how, in the seconds after the execution, he had seen the girl blink her eyelids – how the young surgeon had asked for permission to study every execution since, and had witnessed the same phenomenon again and again.

"A few times –" he took out a small notebook – "seven times, in fact, there have been movements of the lips also. It really is quite affecting. If not speech then a grimace, or a look, sometimes, of surprise."

"Is that not some reflex action?" asked Ezra.

"No, or wouldn't it be the same word? The same action?" Renaud waved his hand, impatient and excited. "The specimens in the laboratory are those that spoke. I am trying to use electricity to enable any consciousness that remains to communicate."

"And has this occurred?" Ezra wasn't sure whether he wanted the answer to be yes or no.

Renaud shook his head. "Not yet. By the time I get the heads back to the laboratory I believe only a tiny spark is left. I have written to the committee about the possibility of setting up a facility on-site, in one of the buildings that line the Place."

"We are sure it is simply a matter of time," Bichat added. Figaud, Ezra noticed, was silent.

The cab stopped, and they got out. The river here was sluggish and still; Ezra could see a great deal of rubbish pushed up against the bank. He turned towards the square, which was thronging with people, men and women, street sellers and pamphleteers offering revolutionary news. Many had the tricolour cockade sewn into their caps, and everywhere small children ran in and out of the crowd.

"You see, friend," Renaud said as he led the way through the press of people, "the advantage of having the Hapsburg emperor and the Hanoverian king – not forgetting the tsar and all his cronies – attempting to quash the revolution, is that there are always plenty of spies to execute."

Suddenly the shouts of the crowd – street vendors crying their wares, mothers shouting at children, singers giving out the latest bawdy tunes – changed, forming into a mass of jeers.

"The sentenced, see?" Bichat pointed. "They have arrived."

It was hard to see above the crowd, but Renaud took hold of Ezra's jacket and practically pulled him through the throng towards the centre of the Place.

"We have the best seats!" he said, close to Ezra's ear.

There were times, as Renaud guided him through the crowd, that Ezra's feet left the ground. He felt hemmed in on all sides, and it was not helped by the smell, of old clothes, of bad teeth, of a thousand stale breaths and a thousand thousand stale tobacco pipes. There were more pleasant scents among them, those of the roast chestnut seller and the potato man, but the stench of the river was overlaid on top of everything.

Eventually Ezra found himself pressed up against some low wooden paling, a sort of fence, and through it he could finally see the centre of the Place, the enormous frame of the guillotine set up upon it. It seemed to stretch ten, twenty feet up into the sky, the blade a dull metal grey. And now Ezra could see the prisoners' cart, open and packed with at least twenty men, women, youths, hands tied behind their backs, in a variety of clothes, some torn, most dirty, faces pale and still with fear. One man was a foot taller than the rest, he wore a pointed beard; another woman, ordinary, wide around the waist, looked close to tears. Ezra noticed a boy, too, barely younger than himself. He wore no jacket, and his thin shirt was torn; he was shivering, from cold or fear or both, but he held himself proudly. His floppy, unkempt blond hair looked as if it had once been well groomed. Another man was clearly gibbering, although it was impossible for Ezra to hear him above the constant hum of the crowd – then someone, somewhere, began to sing. It was the revolutionary anthem, very stirring, far more so than "God Save the King", Ezra thought. Soon the whole crowd had taken it up, and some of the prisoners too. Could they all be evil counter-revolutionaries? Ezra wondered. Every one?

He turned to Renaud, but he had climbed up to the guillotine to speak with an official – one of the guards, blue-coated and surly-looking. The man sneered as he watched the prisoners approach, and he seemed to Ezra as far from the brave young men of the American Regiment as it was possible to be.

The singing was growing louder and more ragged.

In autumn, in the skies of London, vast flocks of starlings swooped and turned so tightly packed you might have imagined them one creature. Ezra was well aware a mob of people could turn as fast as those birds, and there was something brewing, he was sure of it, in this crowd. He looked away from the guillotine, out across the square towards the river, where an enormous plinth – he assumed there had been a statue of some king or other upon it at one time – stood vast and empty. Some youths were scaling it, and he noticed one amongst them, small, wiry, a tricolour rosette on his cap like everyone else in the crowd – but his hat was pulled down and a scarf wrapped round the bottom of his face so only a strip remained clear for his eyes.

The youth threw something with a clear aim, straight at the guillotine, where Renaud and the official were talking. Renaud only just ducked in time. The crowd roared with laughter.

One of the soldiers aimed his rifle up into the air, there was a shout and instantly the singing and laughing all stopped. There was a loud crack, and the gun's retort echoed around the Place. Somewhere a baby cried.

Renaud nodded, the official turned back to the guillotine, and the prisoners were led from the cart.

Ezra wondered about the youth on the plinth. But he had gone.

The first prisoner was the bearded man. Ezra could see where the rope that bound his hands had rubbed the skin raw.

"Look closely!" Renaud called to Ezra, as if he were about to witness a miracle. Ezra swallowed. He must keep an open mind, a scientist's mind. He must watch, he must observe.

Ezra saw the man ascend the steps and watched as the executioner – an ordinary man, neither burly nor coarse, but clean-shaven, a warm cravat tucked into a dark navy jacket, more like a secretary than an executioner – directed the man to kneel.

Renaud waved Ezra over. He hesitated, but then went to join him beside the guillotine. He climbed the steps and looked out over the crowd. Ezra felt conspicuous, as if he was more complicit in this than any ordinary observer. He felt the gun under his jacket and wondered if there was anything one single man could do to stop what was about to happen.

Renaud looked cheery. He set down his basket, opened the lid and spoke to the man, who lay his neck across the wooden bed of the awful machine.

"Perhaps," Renaud said, as if he were a customer in a coffee shop, "perhaps if you would like to remember my name and talk to me the instant you feel your head removed from your body?"

The prisoner gave Renaud a poisonous look and was about to spit in the surgeon's face when the executioner motioned Renaud to step back, and suddenly Ezra heard a kind of metallic whistle and the blade flew down at intense speed. The man's head was off in one swift action, severed, blood pumping out into the air in a tremendous red arc. The head rolled into the wicker basket, and Renaud bent down and caught it up in a flash.

"McAdam!" he exclaimed, holding it up. "Look!"

Ezra saw the man's eyelids flutter once, twice, just as

Renaud had said they would.

Renaud was delighted. "See? There is life!" He reached out with his other hand and slapped the still-warm head about the face. Ezra swore the man grimaced, and he almost fell backwards off the scaffold in surprise and awe.

"My God!" Ezra gasped. Renaud was right. He had seen it. There was life there yet.

The next prisoner had climbed the steps – the young man, he could not be more than fifteen. Through the ragged shirt his skin was almost blue. There was a girl with him, they looked very alike – brother and sister, Ezra thought. The girl almost slipped in the slick of blood on the scaffold, and began to weep. How could these two threaten a whole country, a whole people? Ezra felt ashamed. This was absurd.

He looked back at the other surgeons at the foot of the steps. Surely he could not be the only one who felt like this. Figaud was glancing over his shoulder at the crowd; he seemed uneasy.

"Renaud, do you think you are yet ready to leave?" Figaud called.

"Hmm? Ah." Renaud seemed to catch his meaning, glancing out over the audience as the young prisoners were ushered onto the scaffold. "Yes, I think I am. This first head, I am sure, will yield excellent results. Citizen Bichat, Friend McAdam…"

Ezra nodded and made to climb down – he did not wish to see more die, although he had to admit the thought of seeing some kind of remnants of life was an incredible one. Was there something in Renaud's work? Surely

Ezra's distaste was no different from that shown by those who did not understand how much could be learnt by anatomy, who thought dissection bestial and evil when in reality it had taught humanity and medicine so much?

The others seemed to be in a hurry to leave, and with the press of the mob that surrounded them Ezra was suddenly all too conscious of the poor opinion the general public held for anatomists.

There was a shout from the crowd, a surge pushed against the wooden palings and they buckled. In a great heaving rush the crowd were thronging around the platform of the guillotine. Ezra thought he heard a little gasp; when he looked over at the prisoners, the girl was clutching her brother's arm, both of them tense with a nervous anticipation. The guard seemed not to notice, his attention fixed on the heaving crowd, eyes narrowed, hands tight on his gun.

The executioner had gone pale. Next to him, Renaud dropped his basket; the bearded man's head rolled away into the sea of people, making a path through the crowd as they jumped clear.

Bichat looked terrified. "We must get away. Now!"

Renaud was already off the platform and after the head. Ezra jumped down and found himself face to face with the youth he'd seen on the plinth, with the scarf over his face. He had steely grey eyes, and a light thin blade in his hand – a rapier. Ezra blinked. It was just like Loveday's sword.

Before Ezra could think what this meant, the youth leant close and whispered in a voice as English as boiled vegetables, "Ezra McAdam, I have come to save you!"

62

Ezra thought he must be in a dream. That had been a girl's voice, higher and sharper than any boy's, and the eyes...

"*Loveday?* Loveday Finch?"

"Why, you—"

The guard was behind them – but before Ezra could blink, the youth produced a large piece of wood from behind her, flat and longer than a forearm, and smashed it into the man's face. "None other!"

Ezra was suddenly laughing, all around him the crowd seethed and boiled, and he could only thank heaven she was alive, and laughing too, as she dragged him out through the crowd and towards the bridge. Ezra realized they were not alone – they were flanked by the boy and the girl from the cart, still blue with cold, and an older woman, broad, with a stern, narrow face. She was wielding a sword, and Ezra watched as she sliced at a guard that came close. She did not look at all like the type of woman who would use a sword – she had the look of someone used to comfortable living, although her face was pinched and angry.

Loveday began to run, and she dragged Ezra after her. "Loveday, where are we going?" Ezra looked frantically around for the surgeons, but the little group had now left the Place altogether and they were too far away to see them. "Loveday, wait!"

"Don't talk. There is a tunnel down at the Quai d'Orsay, across the bridge. You will be safe there. Quite safe." The scarf had slipped. It was her! This was no dream.

"No, you don't understand! I do not need saving. On the contrary..."

Ezra looked behind for a split second. The crowd had turned, just like a flock of starlings, and was bearing down towards the bridge, the soldiers in the group at the front stopping to load their guns.

Ezra looked at Loveday. "I assure you, Miss Finch –" Ezra's lungs were fit to burst – "I was perfectly safe a minute ago. Now, it seems, the whole of Paris is after us!"

There was a flash and a bang and a smell that Ezra recognized from the battlefield, gunpowder and smoke. He looked at Loveday in a panic – had she been hit? No, but beside her he saw the boy had stumbled, and the girl at his side let out a cry.

"Carlo!"

"Those sons of dogs," snarled the woman, glancing over her shoulder.

"It is nothing," Carlo gasped, pulling his tattered shirt over his chest where the bullet had hit him.

"We must stop," said Ezra. "I can treat him."

"We can't stop now, boy," the woman said, and Ezra could see the concern in the lines of her face in spite of her stern tone. "They're right behind us – if we stop now, we're all dead."

Chapter Five

The Catacombs
Paris
21 March 1793

Ezra had been running for so long that his legs felt like the bones had been removed and filled with jelly. He no longer had any idea where he was. He and Loveday, along with the escaped prisoners and the stern-looking woman with the sword, rounded what looked like an old warehouse, and then suddenly they were in a tunnel that smelt of dirt and earth and death.

"Where are we?"

"Old mine workings!" Loveday said. "Catacombs! Come on."

"Carlo! Oh, Carlo!" That was the girl. She sounded agitated, and as breathless as Ezra felt.

"I am quite well," Carlo panted. Ezra thought he was a good liar. "Miss Finch – Loveday – you say your companion is a surgeon?"

"Only the best in London."

"Good. There, Maria, I will be all right. Those damned Jacobins will not cut me down." He coughed then, and by the sound of the cough, thick and syrupy,

Ezra imagined he was bringing up blood.

"*Arrêtez*. We will be safe here." It was the woman; Ezra stumbled into her outstretched arm in the dark. "Go on then," she said. "You can treat him, can't you?"

Ezra could feel Carlo's blood, hot and sticky, and he tried to compress the wound, but it was too big, under the ribs. It was a miracle the boy was still on his feet.

"I – I will try," Ezra said. This was not the grey dark of the barn on the Belgian front, this was absolute and utter blackness. He could not even see his hand in front of his face. His master, Mr McAdam, used to say a surgeon should be able to see with his fingertips – but it was no good, the wound was too ragged.

He whispered to Loveday in English, "What is all this? What in heaven's name are you caught up in now? I assure you I was perfectly safe!"

"Don't be ridiculous, Ezra. Nobody from England is safe here. Now come on, your priority is your patient, is it not?"

Ezra sighed. She was right about that at least. "Then we have to get the patient somewhere I can see, and fast. And I need instruments, my own are back at the hospital."

"No!" Loveday was vehement. "We can't take him there. Madame Lascelles –" she turned to the woman, speaking French now – "Ezra cannot work in the dark. Is it far?"

Ezra was fluent in French, but he knew he spoke with a noticeable accent – Loveday, on the other hand, might as well have been a native.

Madame Lascelles scoffed. "It is not, but Carlo needs every second we can spare, Miss Finch."

"Then we must hurry, please." Loveday lowered her voice to a whisper. "Keep him alive, Ezra, I beg you."

"I cannot make any promises, Loveday, you know that."

"Do your best. Please."

"And you will explain this madness? Loveday, I was afraid you were dead!"

"All in good time. Carlo needs your help."

The little group shuffled along in the dark until a strip of light ahead grew bigger, and the tunnel sloped up to a flight of stone steps that ended at a metal gate. Ezra could hear the sound of the street in the distance.

Loveday went ahead. "Madame Lascelles! We will not make it as far as the shop with Carlo. He needs to be treated. Now."

The woman hesitated, but then she seemed to reach a decision, and nodded curtly. "We will be safe in St Michel's – it is only a step from here."

Loveday opened the gate, and Ezra blinked in the light. Across the road was a church, windows boarded up, derelict. Under Loveday's direction Ezra supported Carlo across the street and into a door at the side of the building.

Ezra laid the boy down on the cold stone flagging of the church and tore his shirt open. It disintegrated, sodden in blood. Ezra looked at the wound hard – eyes first, then touch, Mr McAdam had always said. But there was so much blood. It was worse than he had imagined. The bullet had entered his body just under the diaphragm, and at exceptionally close quarters. Even if Ezra had brought his knives, he could neither remove the bullet nor close up the wound. He tried to make a compress as best he could, shaping the rag of the boy's shirt and pressing it over the entry point. He indicated to the girl to take over. It was useless, but at least it was better than inaction, than just watching the boy's life ebb away.

Ezra stood up and signalled to Loveday, and the two of them moved away from the group. She had taken her cap off and Ezra could see her red hair cropped short. There were dark rings round her eyes, which served to make her pale skin look all the whiter. And her face was gaunt; she needed feeding up. Ezra wished they were both at home, safe in London; he would have told her to take to bed and not get up for a week, then he would have had Mrs Boscaven bring her hot chocolate and warm toast.

Loveday smiled at him, and there was for a second the old wild girl there, under the anxiety. There was a chip in her front tooth, but it was, he thought, only endearing.

"I can tell it's bad news, Ezra McAdam," she said in English. "I can read your face like a book."

Ezra kept his voice low. "There is nothing I can do. Even if I had my knives, I cannot remove the bullet. What's more, I believe his lung has collapsed. And he's lost too much blood."

Loveday was ashen. "No, you have to save him. You have to! I owe these people my life. Carlo would never have been taken if it wasn't for me."

"I thought these people were enemies of the revolution?"

Loveday looked close to tears. "What, and that means you shouldn't help them?"

"That's not what I meant!" hissed Ezra. "I don't care

for my patients' politics. You know me better than to think otherwise." He softened. "You know if I could…"

He took her hand but she pulled away.

"Carlo doesn't deserve any of it. He cares only for the circus and for freedom. He is loyal to his friends, not to stupid ideals."

"Loveday, I am sorry for your friend."

"I don't believe that! I saw you, with those black-clad crows. What were you doing? Talking to dead men? Perhaps trying to encourage posthumous confessions?"

"Of course not!" Ezra frowned. It would be pointless to try to explain Renaud's experiments. "Loveday, I do not want to argue with you."

The girl, Maria, sat over Carlo, moving the hair from his now porcelain-white and bloodless forehead. Ezra made his way back over to the pair and felt for the boy's pulse; it was weaker with the second. He tried to make him comfortable, took his own jacket and laid it over him.

The older woman looked angry. She glared at Ezra. "You! American. Do your work."

The boy began to shiver, his teeth chattering. He looked from Ezra to his sister. "I think I am for it, Mother Lascelles. Maria, Loveday – Miss Finch – come close, I beg you."

"Carlo," said Loveday, "I am here. Ezra? Please. Help him."

"There is no more I can do. I am sorry."

The youth tried to answer, but all that emerged was a kind of deep cough, almost a gargle. Ezra knew that sound. He felt for a pulse, but there was nothing. He looked at Loveday, shook his head.

Maria gasped. "No!"

Loveday took the boy's hand in hers. Maria began to cry.

Madame Lascelles stared down at Carlo's body, a look of anger and dismay spreading over her face. All of a sudden she picked up the rapier and brandished it at Ezra.

"You are with the Jacobins, I saw you! You put your thumb into the wound and doubled its size in the dark, no doubt!"

Ezra stood up, but the blade nicked him on the neck. Loveday sprang up at once, and disarmed the woman.

"I trust Ezra McAdam with my life," she declared. "He would never betray me." She paused. Ezra saw Madame Lascelles glaring at Loveday in response, and was surprised that Loveday looked away first. Loveday spoke softly. "He is a good man."

Ezra felt the scratch on his neck, but, mercifully, it was only a scratch. The woman was clearly mad.

Madame Lascelles glowered and turned away, and for a moment there was silence except for Maria's sobs. The girl had thrown her arms around her brother's dead body, her shoulders shaking with grief. The boy's spirit, that spark of life, had gone. He was only flesh and bones. Ezra caught himself wondering what Renaud could do in such a case. Was there really a chance that consciousness, life, remained in the brain, that people did not need their bodies? Ezra swallowed. What kind of life would that be? But, but... There could be so many opportunities, to discover so much about the very edge of existence. Surely that made Renaud's work worthwhile?

Loveday frowned at him, and for a moment Ezra

wondered if she knew what he'd been thinking. Then she turned and slipped out of a door at the far end of the chapel.

Ezra would have run after her, but Maria was sobbing more loudly now and he tried to console her with the empty words that doctors often used. Saying them in French felt a little awkward, but he did what he could – until Madame Lascelles came and stood between them with a stern look at Ezra. He could tell when he wasn't welcome, so he backed away from the tableau of mourning and went after Loveday.

Behind him, Maria began to sing very quietly and softly.

Beyond the door, stone stairs curved up, and Ezra followed them. When he reached the top he pushed open another door that led on to the flat roof of the church tower. Out here the afternoon sky was bright blue, and he could hear the sounds of a market, the trundle of carts and the hooves of horses: familiar, reassuring.

And there was Loveday, looking out across the city smoking a pipe. Ezra almost laughed, partly with relief – she was alive, even if she did look like a caricature of a boy, with her posture, the pipe.

The sun was on her face, and he stood next to her, rolled his sleeves down – then, seeing the blood, rolled them back up again.

"Smoking is not the panacea, you know."

"It adds to the picture," she said. "I have only been wearing boys' clothes for the past few days. I am making an effort to be masculine."

"It is hard to take, I must admit. The hair especially."

"Carlo said I looked like an idiot with no hair." She was trying to be flippant, but Ezra could hear the words catch in her throat.

"Carlo was…" Ezra paused. "A good friend?"

She nodded. "He and Maria both. My father and I used to stay with their family." Loveday looked away. "Mahmoud and I were to stay with them again, but by the time we arrived in Paris, their parents were gone and they were staying with Madame Lascelles – a friend of their parents. She didn't want to take me and Mahmoud in as well, but Carlo insisted."

"I am sorry."

They said nothing for some long minutes. Ezra looked out across the city; through the buildings he could just make out a silver ribbon of water that must be the Seine. He followed the water behind what looked like a large school, then on past the old buildings on the Île de la Cité in the distance, the Cathedral of Notre-Dame, and the hospital beyond.

"I couldn't do anything for him," Ezra said. "If I could have…"

"I know that," Loveday snapped. There was a pause. "All this was only to save him and Maria. The riot, everything."

"*The riot?*" exclaimed Ezra. "Do you mean to say, you caused it?"

"Of course," she said. "We had other friends planted in the crowd – from the circus – to stir up the crowd." Normally Loveday might have sounded proud of that, of pulling off such a tremendous feat, but to Ezra she just sounded tired.

They were quiet again. Ezra could hear the girl, Maria, crying, far away downstairs. Loveday stared into the distance, face set.

Ezra took a deep breath. "Are you very angry with me?"

"I wrote two months ago. Two whole months!" She stared at him.

"I came as quickly as I could!" Ezra said. "The post was delayed. There is a war."

"Hah! That is the excuse for everything – no bread, no money…"

"I was so pleased to see you not two hours ago, and then this is the thanks I get!"

"I lost Mahmoud. I lose everyone. Father, Carlo. Everyone vanishes."

"I do not."

"You are the exception then. I've always believed I can find my way around any problem; I thought I could take Mahmoud back to Turkey. Only now I don't know if he's dead or alive."

Ezra looked at her. This was not like the Loveday he knew.

"When the revolutionaries came for Carlo I couldn't bear it. He's an acrobat, a performer." She looked at him, her eyes moist. "You may be used to death and dying, Ezra McAdam. But I am not. Even after these past months in Paris, I am not." She put her head on his shoulder and threw down her pipe. She sobbed quietly against him, her body shaking, and Ezra did not know what to say.

"Oh, Ez, you would not believe what I have seen…" Her voice trailed off.

Ezra nodded. "I found myself on the Belgian border with the Revolutionary Army. Young men dying all around. You know, once I imagined I would run away to sea, join the navy."

Loveday looked at him, wiped her face on a blue handkerchief she had in her pocket.

"You! On a ship?" She laughed a little. He smiled.

"I know. Ridiculous. A navy sawbones!"

She sighed. "What are we doing here, Ezra?"

He took her hand. The nails were torn and chewed and dirty.

"We are looking for Mahmoud."

"I thought we'd be in Venice by now, or even Constantinople – but we couldn't even afford the ship. We couldn't sell Mahmoud's ruby, I was offered a pittance for it. And I promised him! I promised him I would take him home."

Ezra studied her. At home, in London, she had always been the one who was all certainty and defiance. He hated to see her like this, ground down, anxious.

"We will do it. Together. Wasn't that the old Loveday wading into the heart of the revolution to start a riot? Anyone else would have given up the search, gone home."

"Without Mahmoud? And anyway, do you know how difficult it is to cross the Channel?"

"Of course, but you would have found a way. I did. Remember last year? The Ottoman Embassy?"

She smiled and knitted her fingers into his.

"How could I forget?" Her smile faded. "You know, from here and now, those memories seem like a holiday."

"Even when we were running for our lives?"

"I still am, Ezra. So are Maria and the others. That fire was not an accident. It's not easy being English in this city."

She was right. "Come back with me, Loveday," Ezra said. "You will be safer with me at the hospital, and it will be far easier to look for Mahmoud from there. My friends will be able to help."

She looked at him as if he was an idiot. "Don't you remember? This morning I started a riot. Your doctors were there, Ezra!

"You were disguised, Loveday. I swear if we can find you a dress they will not suspect a thing. I will tell them I got lost in the crowd—"

"And that you simply chanced to run into me afterwards?"

"Why not?" said Ezra. "You might have been attending the execution, and when you are not covering your face with a scarf and dressing as a boy, you are rather hard to miss."

Madame Lascelles was keener than Ezra expected to see them go. She had struck him as the type of woman who would not take kindly to ideas she had not thought of herself, but she seemed to think the plan a good one, and even offered Loveday one of her own dresses to complete the transformation.

"I have several I no longer wear back at the shop," she said bitterly. "I would have tried to sell them, but since hell has come to earth people no longer have money for such things."

Maria looked up from where she was still kneeling by

Carlo's body. "You are returning to the shop?" Her face was streaked with tears. "I will stay here, with Carlo. I would … I would take more time to say goodbye."

"Of course," said Madame Lascelles brusquely.

Maria stood, brushing down her skirts. "Loveday." She took the other girl's hand. She seemed uneasy, and Ezra thought for a moment that it was more than just grief over her brother's death. She glanced over her shoulder at Madame Lascelles, and lowered her eyes. "I hope we will meet again, before you leave Paris," she said quietly.

"So do I," said Loveday. "Maria, I am sorry…"

Madame Lascelles placed a hand on Maria's shoulder. "I will return soon, Maria. Please, be strong."

Madame Lascelles owned a milliner's shop in the north of the city, now closed down, and it was there, in a cramped back room, that she, Loveday and the Franconis had been staying since the fire. Ezra remained on the street outside while the women went in to find a suitable dress, but what he glimpsed of the inside of the shop before Madame Lascelles closed the door behind them was cluttered and dusty. The windows were boarded up. Clearly it had been some time since Madame Lascelles had done any business.

Ezra leant against the windowsill and looked up and down the street. There were many other shops like this one, bedecked with signs that promised fine gloves, perfume and lace. But the revolution no longer needed luxuries, and despite the fine weather the street was nearly empty except for some children grubbing in the gutters and a hungry-looking dog.

The Loveday who emerged from the milliner's shop in one of Madame Lascelles' old dresses was a different one entirely from the one who had gone in wearing trousers. The dress was not a fine one, but it did not need to be – it only needed to be a dress. "What do you think?" She stood in front of Ezra, pulling her chemise straight and then fastening the hooks that held the coarse woollen bodice tight over the top.

Ezra looked. He hesitated; Mrs Boscaven said it was better never to upset a woman by commenting on her dress. "The colour, that blue, it suits you."

Loveday smoothed the bodice down where it fitted close to her waist and pulled the skirts straight. "There."

Ezra was confident that the surgeons would not recognize her. All her possessions were wrapped in one silk handkerchief, apart from her rapier, which she insisted on wearing tied onto a bit of rope around her waist, tucked into her petticoats, and she wore a revolutionary cap for good measure.

"You had better be on your way." Madame Lascelles was standing in the doorway.

Loveday hesitated. "What about Carlo?"

The old woman's expression was solemn. "We will see that he is buried. *Au revoir*, Mademoiselle Finch."

"I am sorry," said Ezra again, but Madame Lascelles only gave him an uncharitable look and retreated into the dusty shop.

"I used to like a good dress," said Loveday as they walked back towards the river and the Hôtel-Dieu. "I had a green one once, when we played in Rome – that was my favourite. Only I'd forgotten how heavy the damned things are."

Ezra smiled. The casual complaining was familiar, and with Loveday at his side he felt a little less like all was lost. Dresses did look unwieldy, it was true, and for a moment he wondered to himself how it had come about that men and women wore such different clothes. Surely for practicality's sake…

They turned into a boulevard, wide and tree-lined with modern buildings stuccoed white, and Ezra saw a different city: this was the Paris he'd imagined. Loveday, though, still looked grim. If he could just cheer her up a little – as the thought struck him, he remembered the gun.

"I almost forgot!"

"What?"

"I have a present. For you. But it will have to wait."

Loveday linked her arm into his. "Excuse my long face." She sighed. "It has been a difficult day."

"You, my dear, are the mistress of the understatement."

"Are you laughing at me?" Loveday clapped him playfully on the shoulder.

As they walked, she explained how she had last seen Mahmoud over two months ago.

"The mood on the streets began to change, and we made a strange pair, an English girl and a Turkish boy. Everyone was – is – scared of foreigners. They thought we were spies. When we came to the Franconis' house and there was no one there, I was afraid we would be left to wander the streets. It was lucky that we found Carlo and Maria at all."

"Where *did* you find them?" asked Ezra.

"At the Cirque-Olympique. They used to perform there as acrobats with their parents."

"And Mahmoud's true identity, you hadn't told a soul?"

Loveday scoffed. "What, that here was the son of the sultan of all Turkey hiding in a lodging house next door to a baker's, en route to his palace in Constantinople? I am not so dim-witted." She made a face and hiked her skirt around to lift it out of the way of a puddle. "How could you think I would do such a thing? But you know Mahmoud," she continued, frowning. "I warned him to act more, well, humble. The Franconis may be royalists – I think their parents supported the old king – but they are not idiots."

"Are you saying they *did* know who he was?"

"I'm not sure!" She sighed again. "Look, Ezra, even if they did, even if perhaps they put one and two together, Carlo and Maria were my friends! They wouldn't have told. If they had, don't you think it would be all over town by now? A sultan's son in Paris? There are a hundred pamphleteers all printing the choicest titbits of news they can find and some of them making up their own. It would be a real coup."

Ezra agreed. And Loveday was right about Mahmoud, too: he was neither restrained nor modest.

It was getting dark when they crossed the Pont Neuf under the shadow of the Palais de Justice and made for the river gate. The old man recognized Ezra and let them in without an argument this time, and they hurried up to Ezra's room.

"I will talk to Bichat. He will not mind you staying

here, I am sure – especially when I explain you were the girl I thought was dead."

"You have a bed? Oh! With sheets and blankets!"

"Loveday, it is yours. I have to find Messieurs – sorry, Citizens – Bichat and Renaud, they will be worried, they may even think me some kind of spy too."

"And they'd be half right. You helped a boy escape the guillotine!"

"Helped?" exclaimed Ezra. "You abducted me! Anyway, it will be simple enough to say I was lost in all the chaos."

"I never would have believed it, Ezra McAdam – the lies drip so easily from you now. When I first met you, I doubted if you even knew how!"

"Loveday, I am trying to save both our skins. They trust me. Not only because I am a surgeon, but I was with the army in the north; I have helped the war effort—" He suddenly remembered. "And I was supposed to deliver Lieutenant Colonel Dumas's letter! By hand!"

"You aren't getting away just yet," Loveday said. "You promised me a present." She looked around the room, and her eyes lit upon the sword. She picked it up and turned it over in her hand, admiring the workmanship, the bronze guard, the red silken tassel.

"This is superb." She looked along the blade and slashed at the air excitedly.

"That is not your present. Although you may have it. I thought your current blade was so special that you would not want another."

"One can never have too many swords. Although apparently they have made duelling illegal in France.

I never heard of such a thing."

Ezra took out the pistol. "So you shan't want this as well? I had it on me earlier but imagined I might somehow inflame the situation if I started waving that about."

"Heavens!" Loveday was completely and utterly speechless. She sat down upon the bed and cradled the gun carefully.

Ezra smiled. "You're pleased, I take it? There are some balls for it in my case. But for pity's sake refrain from firing it inside. Now you must sleep. We can renew the search for Mahmoud tomorrow, and in the meantime I will find my friends. No doubt there is another billet for me somewhere in this vast hospital. You will be safe here, surrounded by your very own arsenal."

He paused. "I am sorry," he said, "honestly and from the heart, about your friend's death. And I am so glad to have found you. If you are alive – and I was so afraid you were dead, burnt to a crisp in that house – then I do not doubt we can find our friend Mahmoud."

Loveday looked back at him. "I want to believe you, Ezra McAdam. But this city –" she shook her head – "I do believe it is the most dangerous place on earth."

Chapter Six

M. Bichat's Residence
Rue St Denis
Paris
21 March 1793

Ezra spent a quiet evening with Bichat's family in his modest home a stone's throw from the river. Bichat's wife was still in a state of high anxiety; she had been terrified their English guest had been swept away with the mob. Ezra assured her he had merely got lost in the crowd running from some youth with a sword, who in turn had seemed to be running from the entire Paris militia – and that he had managed to finally locate his missing friend, news which pleased Bichat, who had clearly been concerned that Ezra's distress over Loveday would ruin his visit.

When supper was over, Ezra managed to put Loveday, safe and sound at last, to the back of his mind, and he passed a pleasant hour with the French surgeon discussing improvements in artery hooks and techniques with difficult patients – was it better to disable them completely somehow to make them submit to treatment? Perhaps with drink or drugs? Ezra was not sure. And there was the business with fevers contracted so soon after operations. Was there no way these infections could be stopped? How were they introduced to the patient, or were they lying dormant within their body, waiting to flare up? Ezra asked about Renaud's work, too; Bichat seemed certain it was the future.

"So you are saying, sir, that one day we may live on, perhaps without any body at all?" Ezra asked.

Bichat shrugged. "Can any of us know what the future might be? As a boy I never imagined living without a king or queen. I cannot see to the end of this year, let alone any further."

"I would never have believed it, what I saw, this afternoon." Ezra shook his head. "I have been thinking about it all day. Bichat, are you sure that what Renaud does is more than triggering reflexes?"

"It certainly seems to be more than that, do you not agree?" said Bichat. "Perhaps it is not, but if it is…"

"Yes." Ezra frowned. "We would be fools not to investigate it."

Madame Bichat had retired early. Bichat drank rather too much of the brandy and gave several rather long speeches about the revolution.

"The people are giddy without a king," he said. "I worry a new, worse king may come along and quite turn our heads." He smiled sadly. "I am planning to send my wife and the children away, you know? Paris is getting worse." He sighed. "I am sorry. It is only… Even as a surgeon, I have never seen so much death before. I know it is all for a good cause, but…"

Ezra felt sorry for him. He'd seemed so sure of himself just a few months ago in London, at the master's funeral.

But Ezra knew just how much could change in a short time. Hadn't he gone from being an apprentice to living on the street to becoming a surgeon with his own practice in the same period?

Bichat found him a bed in the top of the house and he lay down as the local church struck dully for midnight. He thought about the revolution, about Lieutenant Colonel Dumas's speech in that cold field in Belgium – that yes, some people, those who had an interest in the idea of aristocracy (which to Ezra's mind was an arbitrary system in any case, where power rested with a few thanks to an accident of birth rather than aptitude or consensus), might need some education on the benefit of change. But the removal of anyone's head seemed rather severe. And what did Loveday think she was doing with Madame Lascelles? He would find out tomorrow, he told himself; they would deliver Dumas's letter and they would make steps to find Mahmoud.

Ezra woke early and joined Figaud on his ward rounds at the hospital – it was a short walk from Bichat's house to the Hôtel-Dieu. Ezra had no illusions about city hospitals, and as in London there was a mixture of incurables and inoperables. The smell was worse than St Bartholomew's. Figaud explained that the hospital was designed for five hundred but regularly had to house four times as many. The floors in particular were filthy, Ezra would not have been surprised to see animals rooting around in the dirt, and the bed linen might once have been white but was stained and foul. Everything seemed old and used; it struck Ezra more as a place to die than to recover.

Ezra thought he might check in on Loveday once they had finished their rounds, but Figaud, perhaps sensing that his English colleague had been unimpressed with the state of the wards, insisted that he accompany him to the operating theatre. When they arrived, Ezra could see why: the wards themselves might have been poorly kept, but the operating theatre was as impressive as the laboratory, and while the fittings were not quite as modern, the light was particularly good. Not a glass roof as he had at Great Windmill Street, but plenty of skylights.

Ezra wondered how many patients, having survived an operation here, went on to die on the wards. It reminded him of the battlefield – the amputation was controllable, manageable, but the infections that followed were far less so.

Figaud left him to prepare for the session, and Ezra entered the theatre through a door at the top, where he could see straight down to the table in the centre. There were two sets of stairs down to the bottom, and the seats were steeply racked. They were practically all taken – the crowd, medical students and interested onlookers, smoked and talked. Then Figaud appeared through a door at the back dressed in a leather apron and the room fell silent. Ezra craned to look round the fellow in front of him and saw a boy bound on the table, one poor mangled foot strapped into place. His eyes were wild with terror and the sweat on his forehead glistened. He was yelling and swearing for all he was worth.

Ezra recognized the boy's voice, and he realized with a start that it was Luc, the street urchin he'd met yesterday.

"*Non!* I have changed my mind! I'm not ready to

be the one-legged beggar of the streets!" Luc begged Figaud. "The foot will heal. I may limp, but at least…"

Ezra pushed forward through the crowd, trying to reach the stairs.

Figaud leant over and inspected the boy's foot. "You were trampled, yes?"

"*Oui*. In the riot at the execution. Felt like the whole world came down on it!"

Figaud reached out and touched what was left of one of the boy's toes, and Luc screamed.

Figaud looked serious. "If we leave this rotten, degraded flesh and bone, there is an overwhelming chance of gangrene taking hold and killing you." His tone was not wholly without sympathy, but matter-of-fact nonetheless.

"Get on with it!" one of the onlookers yelled.

Figaud looked up in resigned irritation. "This is no sideshow, citizen, this is medicine."

Ezra had now made his way to the front row, "Luc! Luc!"

"American!" Luc exclaimed, but then he saw that Figaud had his knives out, and all the colour drained out of him. "No! Let me go. Let me out of here now. You will chop me up and feed me to the sewer rats. I can't just grow another foot! *Laissez-moi partir!*"

"Luc," Ezra said calmly. "Monsieur Figaud means you no harm."

"No harm? American, I am to lose my left foot! I am crippled for ever!"

"McAdam!" Figaud said warmly. "This is an interesting procedure; the boy's injuries will make for a textbook

Chopart amputation." Luc wailed. "See, McAdam, I will take off the lower part of the foot, merely the toes and another inch or so. Here through the midtarsal joint..." He traced a line above the damaged toes.

Luc squirmed. "American! Stop him, Mister!"

Figaud must have been used to the cries of distressed patients, but his bedside manner could use some work, in Ezra's opinion. He considered interjecting, but Figaud went on, "The ankle will remain, and the heel. There will, no doubt, be a difficulty with his balance until he is accustomed to it."

Ezra looked at the mangled, flattened foot. It resembled nothing so much as a steak beaten flat for ease of cooking. Only this steak contained bones.

"It is the best option?" Ezra asked.

"For certain." Figaud nodded.

Ezra reached to grip the boy's hand. Luc looked at him, panicked, but said no more. His mouth opened in a scream as Figaud began his work, quickly and deftly, parting the flesh of the foot as if it was warm butter. Ezra could not help but admire his skill as the skin was peeled back and the crushed muscle and bone discarded – although if he had performed the operation himself he would have kept more skin, to make a good-sized flap to cover the wound, instead of putting in quite so many stitches as Friend Figaud. It had been McAdam's belief, and Ezra's too, now he thought of it, that stitches, even of quality cat gut, the kind Figaud used now, could cause problems later. Still, Figaud's needlework was superb and the wound looked clean and healthy. It was a good job, Ezra thought.

There was a round of polite applause from the gathered audience; as Figaud tidied up, a few approached him to ask questions. Luc, for his part, was out cold, having fallen into unconsciousness as Figaud had begun to saw through the bone.

"Would you join me for lunch, McAdam?" said Figaud cheerfully.

"Actually," Ezra said, "if you don't mind, I'd like to speak with the boy – I met him the day I arrived and he was very helpful indeed. I don't believe he has any family."

"Ah – it is all too common with these children," said Figaud. "Very well. You know where to find me, yes?"

Ezra nodded, and he accompanied Luc's unconscious body as he was carried to a bed in the overcrowded ward near by.

It was a while before the boy woke up, and his face immediately twisted into a grimace of pain. Ezra smiled all the same. "There you are."

"That man! That devil!" Luc tried to sit up.

"Keep still; the stump will still be sore, but it was done brilliantly. You will thank him – Citizen Figaud – mark my words."

Luc began to cry. "I will not! What will I do now? How will I earn a *sou* like this? *Hein?* Answer me that! Not everyone hands out francs like Americans. What's the joke about a one-legged boy?" He looked furious. "I'll tell you – there aren't any."

Ezra was calm, and he tried to sound kind. "It's your foot, not your leg, and you still have half of it."

Luc ignored him. "Come to think of it, this –" he

pointed at his foot – "this is all your fault!"

"What? How's that?"

"If you had never handed me those two francs I would have been down by the river yesterday where the diligences come in, waiting for travellers, not having a holiday at the Place watching the aristos snuff it!"

Ezra shifted in his wooden chair. "You are upset, that is natural. You have experienced a deep trauma."

"'Trauma'? *Qu'est-ce que c'est?* You, American, you owe me for the rest of my life!"

Ezra did his best to assure the distraught boy that all would be well – different, but well. He did not mention that many died after operations, like the soldiers struck down with fever; this was not the time for that. He promised to find Jean and tell him that Luc would recover. As he walked away, he had an idea, and doubled back.

"Have you come to take my other foot? Truly you are the butcher's friend!"

"I am not a butcher." Ezra bit his tongue. The boy was in a state, he reminded himself. The young surgeon sat down, face level with Luc's. "I was wondering…"

"It will cost you."

"I will pay. I will bring you food, three times a day. How about that?"

"I suppose that will be a start. What's the question?"

"Do you live on the streets? You and Jean?"

"Me and a lot more besides. Why?"

"Then you probably see things, notice things…"

"Course. Cut to the chase, *vieillard.*"

Ezra tried not to smile. He had been called many things in his lifetime, but never old.

"The Rue des Enfants Rouges, you said you knew it well?"

"Told you, didn't I?"

"Yes, you did." Ezra nodded. "So, I was wondering if you ever saw a foreign boy, next door to the baker's. The one that burnt down, remember?"

"Dark-haired? Nose in the air?"

Ezra smiled. "Yes! A most perfect summation of the boy in question! He vanished, a few weeks before the fire."

"You want him too, do you? Seems like he was in demand. Heavens knows what he did, too dark-skinned for an aristo. Don't tell me he was an American like yourself!"

"Luc. Tell me, please. What happened to him?"

The boy folded his arms. "I'm not saying anything until I'm paid. I like buns, the ones with currants from the woman with a stall on the Quai d'Orsay." Luc shut his eyes and tried to roll over, but the pain in his foot stopped him.

Ezra got up. "Buns it is."

He almost ran out of the ward – wait until Loveday heard this! – and flew across the gardens and up the steps to her room.

"Ezra!" she exclaimed, spinning around in a whirl of skirts as he opened the door. "You might have knocked! I think I slept past breakfast. And what if I'd still been dressing?"

Ezra felt his face flush. "I'm sorry, Loveday, but I have news about Mahmoud—"

"News?"

"Well – almost. Come with me and I'll tell all."

As they descended the stairs he explained how his new friend Luc had claimed he'd seen Mahmoud, and that if they went out and purchased some buns for the boy they might finally have some answers. Loveday was ready to leave at once, but as they made their way across the gardens they were interrupted.

"McAdam!" It was Renaud. "So good to see you. Citizen Bichat told me you had made it back safely, but I was, nonetheless, concerned…" He trailed off, looking at Loveday with something like surprise. "And who is this?"

"This is my good friend Loveday Finch," said Ezra. "She is the one I came to Paris to meet."

"I am pleased to make your acquaintance, *mademoiselle*," said Renaud, executing a rather awkward little bow. Loveday covered her smile with her hand. "I am Samuel Renaud; I am staying at the Hôtel-Dieu to further my experiments into the limits of human life – the edge of consciousness."

"Oh, really?" Loveday was intrigued.

"Yes, it's very interesting," said Ezra quickly. "But Loveday and I are on our way out – I have a letter to deliver, you see, and…"

Renaud seemed quite put out. "I can take care of Miss Finch if you are in a hurry. I have the new specimen, too, from yesterday."

Loveday brightened. "Do you think I could see?"

Ezra made a face at her. "I am not sure."

"Oh, come now, Ezra, I am hardly squeamish. I could handle your laboratory and museum in London perfectly well!"

Which was true, but Renaud's experiments had troubled even Ezra – not that he wanted to say so in front of the man. The problem was, he was certain Loveday wouldn't be so polite.

"Perhaps later," Ezra suggested. "We have someone to find, remember?"

Loveday frowned. "You are right, although it pains me to say it."

"And the trail grows colder and colder," Ezra added.

"Please excuse me," she said to Renaud. "Although I would be most honoured to see your work, it seems it will have to wait." She smiled. "Perhaps another time?"

Renaud seemed a little deflated, but he nodded and made towards his laboratory as Ezra led Loveday towards the gate.

"You would not like it, Loveday. Not one bit." He paused. She looked at him, raised one eyebrow.

"In fact," Ezra admitted, "I am not sure I have made my mind up about it myself."

Loveday looked surprised. "You! According to you, the answer to everything can be found in a laboratory. In that case my interest is well and truly piqued. What does he do? Sew rabbits' feet on poor souls' noses? Transplant tails or extra toes?"

"Loveday, please." Ezra smiled. "Don't say such things in Renaud's hearing, he may just take your words as inspiration."

They hurried out through the gate and into the city, and their conversation turned back to Mahmoud. Ezra told her what Luc had said, about him being in demand, and Loveday frowned. She had been certain no one had followed them from London, none of Ahmat's allies, no scowling Russians. No one. It had been a relief for both of them, she said. "Now I wish we *had* noticed them."

They decided to go first to deliver Dumas's letter. Loveday led the way, as she knew where to find the War Office – it was, she explained, in an old palace near the Tuileries Garden.

"They are trying to change the names of everything these days, it is most confusing," she said. "When I was here with Pa the streets and the buildings all had different names. Even the cathedral is not a cathedral any more."

"The 'Temple of Reason', isn't it?" Ezra asked.

"Yes – although most Parisians forget half the time." She lowered her voice. "This revolution is utter madness, but if you venture any opinion against it you are cut down."

Ezra stopped her. "Isn't it a better way, Loveday? A new way, a new system where all are equal and none raised up higher than any other? Where all fight for the good of one another? Isn't that progress?"

Loveday laughed. "Look around. There is no food and they cut off people's heads as if they are chickens to be slaughtered. It is a city where, if you are high-born – by accident, I might add – you are an enemy, an outlaw." She sighed. "Carlo and Maria's parents were always good to me and Pa. They loved our shows. Now they are dead and their children have nothing and hide in a boarded-up shop." She glared, daring him to argue back. "How is that any kind of progress?"

She stalked off ahead, managing to move rather fast

even in her dress. Ezra had to hurry to catch up.

The War Office was large and imposing, taking up an entire block close to the Louvre Palace. Loveday, despite having led Ezra there in the first place, seemed to balk a little at the huge black-painted door.

"I can't go in there. What if they recognize me from yesterday?"

"You were dressed as a boy, Loveday," Ezra whispered, "and running away!"

"My hair is still short!" she insisted. "You should go in without me – this is your errand, anyway."

Ezra argued that she might be at least as conspicuous waiting outside, but he bid her wait for him in the courtyard and went in alone. The vast, marble-floored entrance hall was full of people hurrying about, many in uniform, red coats, blue coats, brown leather boots, some shiny, some caked with mud. Ezra stopped what he assumed was a messenger boy at the foot of a palatial curving staircase.

"I am looking for General Le Brun?" He held out the letter.

"General Le Brun's office is on the first floor, facing the street." The boy scurried away, and Ezra sighed. He would obviously have to put it into the man's hand himself.

He took the stairs two at a time, keen not to leave Loveday on her own for too long. The decor was just as smart upstairs, gold embellishments and soft carpet throughout, a contrast to the spartan hospital. He looked up; the chandelier at the top of the staircase was so large, it would take the whole stock of a chandler's shop just to fill it with candles. Ezra smiled, he liked the fact that this vast palace was now owned by the people – he just wished the people didn't need it as a War Office.

Ezra found General Le Brun's office, knocked on the door and entered. Le Brun sat behind a large desk. Apart from the usual inkwell and blotters, on the desk was a shining ceremonial sword balanced on a stand, bright red silken tassels falling from its handle, metal gleaming. It formed such a contrast to the severe dress and scraped-back hair of the man in front of him that Ezra was quite distracted by the sight.

Le Brun smiled. "Magnificent, isn't it? Belonged to the comte." He paused. "Let's simply say I won it, in a duel." He broke out of his reverie and looked Ezra up and down. "What is your business?"

"I am a surgeon," Ezra began, also in French.

"You? A surgeon?" Le Brun stood up and Ezra wished he'd held his tongue.

"Yes, sir."

"Citizen. It is *citizen*."

"I'm sorry, citizen. I am a surgeon; I was briefly with the American Regiment, and Lieutenant Colonel Dumas bid me deliver this letter."

Le Brun studied Ezra. "I didn't realize we were training you fellows up to wield knives."

Ezra bristled. "I have trained all my life, sir, under the best surgeon in the world in the best city." He hesitated. There would be no value at all in revealing his Englishness. "In Edinburgh, in Scotland." He knew the French felt nothing but affection for the Scots.

Le Brun nodded. "Edinburgh. I suppose that accounts

for your accent, which I'd assumed was that of a colonialist. But Edinburgh is so far north it is a wonder your kind could concentrate in such cold."

Ezra tightened his lips. He had hoped a revolution would have swept away such old-fashioned and unscientific thinking. He put the letter down on the desk but Le Brun did not pick it up.

"Dumas said it was urgent. I would have delivered it sooner." Ezra was babbling, and the general seemed to be enjoying his discomfort. Ezra calmed himself; he was a dignified surgeon and as good as any.

"You will read it?" he said. "Only Dumas was worried, about supplies for the regiment – armaments, uniforms, boots…"

Le Brun gave Ezra a look that was openly hostile. He leant forward, jabbing a finger towards him as forcefully as Loveday wielded her sword.

"A lieutenant colonel should not be discussing matters and circumstances of the Revolutionary Army with a foreigner. He risks his men, he risks the new French state. The man is a loose cannon," he sneered. "And you may well be an *Américain* but I assure you this is not your business. Is that clear?"

Ezra stepped back, indignant. "Lieutenant Colonel Dumas wants only victory! I saw him fight; he took on an entire enemy platoon with only a handful of men. France should be proud!"

Ezra realized too late he had said too much.

Le Brun scowled. "I do not need a foreigner to tell me when my country should be proud. I will hear no more!" He walked to the door and opened it. "You will leave.

Thank you for the letter. I would hope that you will keep these facts to yourself unless you too would be an enemy of the revolution." He ushered Ezra out into the corridor and abruptly shut the door.

Ezra felt a sudden chill. How could anyone believe Dumas was against the revolution? Surely Le Brun would send those supplies!

He stood for a moment, trying to understand exactly what had happened. Then he remembered Loveday waiting for him – and somewhere, too, he hoped, Mahmoud. Surely, he told himself, the soldiers of the American Regiment were fierce enough to look after themselves.

Chapter Seven

The Place des Victoires
Paris
22 March 1793

Ezra came out of the War Office and stood on the steps, scanning the square. The buildings here were fine, not far off new, and stuccoed like those in the more modern parts of London. There were a few trees scattered about, with buds of pale pink blossom light against the black bark. Here, one could almost pretend the turmoil of the rest of the city did not exist – but Ezra could not shake off his concerns about Mahmoud, nor indeed the distinctly uncomfortable feeling with which his meeting with Le Brun had left him.

But there was nothing more he could do for Lieutenant Colonel Dumas now. He tried to put the unpleasant encounter to the back of his mind, and looked around for Loveday.

He did not see her at first and his stomach turned over. What if she'd said the wrong thing? What if someone had denounced her as a spy? But then he noticed a knot of street children crowding around a low wall at the side of the square. In the centre of the throng was Loveday

Finch. What was she doing? Was she being mobbed? Arrested?

He ran over quickly, and saw the children erupt into squeals of delight and laughter as she made a rather faded red handkerchief appear magically from her mouth. And then, just as suddenly, she scrunched it up in her hands and it was gone. The children watched wide-eyed as she pulled it out of one child's ear, then another's sleeve, and then she seemed to throw it up into the air and it had disappeared once again.

Some of the children gasped. Ezra led the applause. Loveday was smiling, and Ezra, seeing her truly happy for the first time since he'd been in Paris, could not help smiling too.

"I think perhaps I should take up performing again. I hadn't realized how much I miss it." They were walking back through the city to find some currant buns for Luc.

"I shall get myself an assistant – you, of course, will be far too busy slicing people up and sewing them back together again – and be the first and foremost lady magician in the whole world!"

"I would be most happy to endorse you." Ezra gave an elaborate flourish and declared, "Ladies and gentlemen, I give you the fabulous Citizen Finch!"

"And I shall endorse you in return," Loveday replied. "Everywhere I go, from St Petersburg to New York – and I rather fancy New York – I will remind my audience that if they need a leg lopped off, they must go to London and seek out Ezra McAdam!"

They bowed to each other and laughed.

*　　*　　*

"We will find him," Ezra said, later, when they turned into a street of small shops and stalls that gave on to the Quai d'Orsay. He bought a bag of buns from a baker's stall, and then the two of them hurried back to the hospital.

"I bet if you show Luc some magic he'll tell us more," Ezra said.

Loveday sighed. "I hope so. I have racked my brains to think what might have happened to Mahmoud. The last day I saw him, I went out to sell the ruby and arrange onward transport to the south – the plan was to go overland to Italy, then take a boat from Venice. I told him a thousand and one times to stay put. But when I returned…"

"He is resourceful, for a prince," Ezra reminded her. "He lived rough on the streets of London all through last winter, with the Russians after him too."

Loveday nodded, although she still looked a little too hopeless for Ezra's liking. "Don't pin all your dreams on this street boy's testimony, though, Ez. I know many of those children would sell you the old cathedral for a bowl of custard."

They cut through a market, which wasn't so much a market as a street where people had rolled out blankets and set out the sum of their possessions for sale. It was quite fun at first; Loveday tried on a hat that was far too big, and Ezra found himself a good winter jacket which he almost bought before he reminded himself that spring was on the way. There were chairs that were slightly broken, plates with cracks, a pile of dresses and underthings, old boots and table linen, lamps, bundles of cutlery tied with twine. Then they came to some workmen selling their tools. Weary-eyed men selling awls and hacksaws; others spades and rakes. It was not only sellers of frivolities like Madame Lascelles whose livelihoods had suffered from the revolution.

Ezra felt his heart sink. He looked at Loveday; he could tell she felt the same. He reached for her hand and gave it a squeeze, and they hurried away towards the river.

They found Luc in the paupers' ward, sitting up in bed. Ezra made a face, he could see there was no space to lie down as there were three other people squashed together in with him. One man sat next to Luc reading a pamphlet that foretold the end of the world. At the other end two more slept: an old man snoring deep in sleep, his nose scarred by the pox; the other tossing and turning and groaning.

Loveday covered her face with a handkerchief. The stench of sickness and death was as thick as a night soil-man's cart. Ezra felt the restless man's forehead; he was running a high fever, burning up. Ezra frowned. What if the fellow's fever was transmittable?

What could he do? There were six beds in this ward, and over twenty patients stuffed three or four or even five to a bed. He had told Luc he would recover. How could anyone get better in this place? He glanced over to where the ward nurse was sitting by the fire smoking a pipe. She did not seem to have even noticed they were there.

Ezra made a decision and gathered Luc up in his arms, careful of his foot as he did so.

"What are you doing, American?" the boy asked.

"Looking after you," Ezra answered. "And we have buns."

Luc relaxed, grinning, and with Loveday trailing behind, Ezra took the boy out and away from the poor wards, up the stairs and into the small, plain room where Loveday had slept.

Ezra laid him down. "In my bed?" Loveday hissed, more than a little annoyed. "Do you plan to treat each one of the Hôtel-Dieu's patients in this room?"

Before he handed over the buns, Ezra checked Luc's wound. Still clean, and still painful. While he did so, he asked Loveday to produce and vanish the handkerchief in order to distract the boy. Luc's jaw duly dropped.

"I saw a man do something like that the Easter before last in Tarbes, back home. But I never saw a girl do magic, not in all my days. Do it again, *mademoiselle*, please!"

Ezra retied the bandage and produced the buns. "You tell us what you saw – remember, the boy, dark-skinned but not as dark as me?"

Luc tore his eyes away from Loveday. "Do they have currants?"

"The baker swore blind there's fruit in them."

Luc looked hard at Loveday. "I have seen you before, haven't I? You were there, living in the Rue des Enfants – no, Hommes Armés, or whatever it's called these days." He turned to Ezra. "She's the one you thought was dead, that's it!" He smiled broadly at Loveday. "Only you had a deal more hair. More like a girl's hair, and the colour! Jean said you must wash it in cow's piss to make it like that. I said that it just grew out of your head. I'm right, aren't I?"

Loveday was indignant. "My hair is completely

natural! It has never been anywhere near cow's—"

Luc was triumphant. "I knew I was right! Wait till I tell Jean. Did you see him? Is he outside waiting for me?"

"No," said Ezra, feeling a little guilty that he had not thought to look. "But I promise that when I see him, I will tell him where you are. Now, please, this boy, he's been missing for days and he doesn't know the city. Did you see him?" Ezra held out a bun, which Luc swiped out of his hand as if he was afraid it might be taken away again.

"With her," he pointed at Loveday. "Yes."

"And never alone?" Loveday asked.

The boy paused, screwed up his face in thought. "No. Wait! Yes." Ezra and Loveday were both staring now.

"Go on!"

"Well, *I* wasn't the one who saw him, but I remember Jean telling me his friend had seen him. It was the day I found that good woollen coat. I said it was from Normandy but Jean said it was from the mountains, like him, and I said—"

"Cut to it!" Loveday said impatiently.

"All right, all right! I said to Jean, 'I haven't seen that posh *garçon* around today,' and Jean said that his friend Rémy had seen him the night before, getting marched off westwards by a man and a woman, shouting himself hoarse in some foreign tongue—"

Loveday sat up. "What? Someone took him? That's not possible! Never. Ezra, there was no sign of a break-in, none at all!"

Ezra handed Luc another bun. "Did Jean's friend say anything about the people he was with?"

"A man and a woman, like I said. One of them, he

said, was that young man, the one where you lived –" he nodded to Loveday – "next to the baker's, and the other one was a broad old woman."

Loveday paled. "No. He must have been mistaken."

Luc shook his head, taking a bite out of the bun. "Rémy's all right, but he's too dim to make up something like that. He said it was that young man with the floppy hair – Jean said he must be posh because only nobs have floppy hair like that because it doesn't matter if it gets in the way of what they're doing."

Ezra noticed Loveday swallow. "I think this boy doesn't know what he sees," she said in English.

He could see she was hiding something. He felt suddenly betrayed. "Loveday, tell me the truth."

She looked away. Luc went on, "He said they had a cab at the end of the road and they pushed the kid into it, whether he liked it or not. They all went in it together, the three of them."

Luc held out a hand and Ezra gave him a third bun. The boy tore into it and it vanished quicker than any handkerchief.

Loveday stood up. "Carlo wouldn't. He wouldn't…"

Luc shrugged. "Well, that's what I heard. Wasn't he a friend of yours, that *fils*? Didn't they tell you all about it? Don't you never talk to each other about what goes on?" As he spoke, he sprayed crumbs.

"Loveday," Ezra said, "it was Carlo he saw!" He was speaking in English again now. "And a broad old woman? That must be Madame Lascelles!"

"I don't believe it. It doesn't make any sense. It can't have been Carlo. That boy must have been making it up."

"Why would he?" hissed Ezra. "It can't be a coincidence!"

"No! They would never!" Loveday stormed out of the room.

Ezra nodded at Luc to thank him, and hurried after Loveday.

Luc called after them, "Oi! Any chance of me getting out of here before they chop me up for sport?"

Ezra caught up with Loveday at the top of the stairs. "Your friends, they must know something! We should go now, to Madame Lascelles' shop, talk to them."

"Mahmoud isn't there. I would have known." Loveday didn't look at him. "I don't believe any of it."

Outside she walked quickly, her arms folded tightly across her chest, her face set in a scowl. "Luc is a beggar. He's stringing you along. It's a magic trick as much as what I do with the handkerchief. Telling the mug what he wants to hear."

Ezra bridled. "Just because he lives on the street doesn't mean he's a liar. I am not a mug."

"Oh, in this case I think you are! Don't you imagine they would have told me if they knew what happened to Mahmoud? I have searched for him for weeks, they watched me go out each day."

Ezra's voice was low, angry. "Exactly. We need to talk to them. We can go now if we get a cab."

"You think I would take you, Mr Citizen Revolutionary, and betray my friends?"

Ezra glared at her. "I thought *I* was your friend. I thought you cared for Mahmoud too!"

Loveday stared back. "I looked after him. I did!

Whatever you think about them, it doesn't make sense. Why would they kidnap him? There's no reason at all."

"But if they had worked out who he was…"

Loveday stopped walking. She lowered her voice. "Carlo and Maria are – were – good people! They wouldn't kidnap anyone, wouldn't know how to. And for heaven's sake, why would they? They are circus performers!"

"Exactly! Circus performers on an uncertain wage in a city of chaos. Can you imagine how much Mahmoud would be worth?"

"I can't believe you, Ezra. That boy would say anything for a bun! Carlo was honourable."

"But what if he *wasn't*?" Ezra insisted. "Loveday, this is the only lead we have!"

Loveday was furious now, face as red as her hair. Ezra would not have been surprised if she had spat fire.

"He was just a young man. He never did any harm to anyone. So you can shut up, Ezra McAdam, because you might know everything there is to know about blood and bones but you don't know anything about human hearts!" Her voice was low and dangerous. She began to march off.

Ezra ran to catch up. "Loveday." He touched her back, and she spun around, sword in hand. He had to step back, put his hands up. She wouldn't cut him, would she?

"Loveday, please!"

She kept her sword up. "Go on, Ezra McAdam, get back to your black crows and your dead people! You can go swing for all I care!"

She turned on her heel and Ezra stood, stunned by the force of her words, as she walked away into the stew of the city.

Chapter Eight

Petit Pont
Paris
22 March 1793

Ezra watched helplessly as Loveday stormed away across the smaller bridge, the Petit Pont, heading south and away into the city. She was almost out of sight before he realized what an utter fool he'd been not to follow her sooner. He rushed after her as fast as he could, through the traffic up the hill that sloped away from the river. He pushed across the street through the carts and carriages, trying to keep a fix on her red bonnet, which seemed to be getting further and further away. Up ahead he saw her take a sharp right turn into what looked like gardens, tall old horse chestnut trees covered in candles of pink and white blossom.

Ezra ran, in and out of knots of students that spilt out of the university buildings, noisily discussing a lecture. Ezra weaved around them, narrowly avoiding collision with street sellers offering trays of hard-boiled eggs or rolls, but as he entered the park he was met by the sight of not one figure but at least fifty men, women and children, all wearing the red revolutionary cap with a tricolour rosette. They were crowded around listening to a speaker standing on the seat of a chair as he told them that priests and nuns were the enemies of the people.

"All of them?" someone shouted.

"All of them!" insisted the man on the chair. "They keep the riches of the church for themselves and watch as men and women starve! The revolution will not allow these injustices! Greed will not go unpunished! We are witnessing the dawning of a new age, citizens!"

Ezra pushed through the crowd, looking from one face to another – she had to be here somewhere.

Half an hour later he still had not found her. It was as if she'd vanished, swallowed up by the flower beds – or more likely back with Madame Lascelles and Maria. Ezra cursed. Why hadn't he paid more attention to the route yesterday? He tried to remember, but the only thing he knew for certain was that they'd been on the south side of the river and the church had been Saint-Michel.

He looked round and felt like an idiot. This place was entirely and completely foreign to him. A city at least as big as London and he could not tell north from south or east from west without looking up at the sun. And even then he still had no idea where he stood, where the centre of this city was, where it was safe and where might be best avoided. He hoped Loveday kept her mouth shut.

He walked round the gardens one more time, past what appeared to be a palace but, by the look of the guards at the tall ironwork gates, seemed to be serving as a prison, and out into another street. He peered up and down, the streets were full, people talking, children laughing, a few playing games up against a wall. A carter with a wagon-load of wood, another leading a mule piled high with hay, a boy wheeling an empty barrow. People were the same everywhere, revolution or no revolution. Life had to go on.

Ezra suddenly felt homesick. He wished he had never left London, and wondered how Josiah and Mrs Boscaven would be managing without him. He wished he could apologize to Loveday. He wished she had listened. More than that, he wished he had an idea of where to find Mahmoud. Who knew what Loveday might do? She was so convinced her circus performer friends were innocent – but if they weren't, if they were lying to her, would she be safe with them? She was a good swordswoman, but there was only one of Loveday, and who knew how many of them. He cursed again. He had to find her! He should have followed more closely, damn it!

The streets were crowded, thronging with people going about their daily business with the casual disregard that came from treading a city's streets one's whole life. Ezra thought of London, and how much simpler it would have been, there, for him to track down an indignant Loveday – or, indeed, a lost prince…

His thoughts were disrupted by a commotion further down the street. A man was shouting, "You have the wrong man! I am Scottish, not English – *la Vielle Alliance!* I came here to help the revolution!"

"It's true! He is innocent!" a woman shouted, stepping forward from the growing crowd, but the militia guard who was restraining the man – Ezra could see his arms were twisted uncomfortably behind his back in the guard's harsh grip – was unmoved.

"Of course he is," he spat. "That's what they all say."

"You can't trust her," called one of the onlookers. "He was staying at her house!" The militia captain, a big man with a bushy moustache and steely eyes, turned to the woman. Her face had turned pale and she started to back away, but not quickly enough. Another one of the guards seized her by the wrist, hauling her almost clear off the ground.

"Harbouring spies, eh? Sounds like another appointment with the guillotine to me."

"No," the woman gasped. "No, *je vous en prie!*"

Ezra had seen enough. Shaken, he hurried away, trying to keep his head down. He knew no one would take him for English with his skin, but he remembered with a queasy feeling how he had told General Le Brun that he had studied in Edinburgh. How much would that be worth to a member of the revolutionary militia?

And what about Loveday? Her French was fluent, but it would take only a small a slip-up…

He needed to find her, and quickly – but he knew he never would, her *or* Mahmoud, without the help of someone who knew Paris.

Ezra took his bearings from the sun, and turned north for the river. If he could find the Seine he'd make it back to the hospital. Would Renaud help him? He couldn't see it. Perhaps Bichat? Ezra sighed and quickened his step.

Then he had an idea, a brilliant one – the Cirque-Olympique! If anyone knew where Maria – and therefore probably Loveday – was, it would be someone there. He needed a cab at least, but even better would be a guide.

Ezra broke into a run, and there through the maze of buildings he saw the river and the imposing towers of Nôtre-Dame, or whatever it was called nowadays. He sped up until he reached the hospital gates and the gatekeeper waved him through like an old friend.

The room was exactly as he had left it; Luc was looking at a pamphlet that had been left by Ezra the night he had slept there.

"Is this any good?" Luc asked. "Are there any jokes? Only I can't read more than the first line."

Ezra sat down. "Luc, listen to me." He was out of breath. "You know the city inside out, don't you?"

"Course! When you've run down every street as often as I have…" Luc's voice trailed off. Ezra could see he was thinking his running days were over.

"I need help. And quickly, as soon as possible. I need to find someone."

"Sir, you seem to lose people as easily as ladies lose hairpins."

"Didn't you say you hated hospitals?"

"Yes, but this room is grand. I don't think I've ever slept in a bed on my own in my life."

"I need to find you some boots or some clogs, for that foot." The boy's face lit up.

"My very own shoes! I'd like leather ones, with buckles maybe. The man who owned the smith in Tarbes, he had buckles for church on Sunday. I used to love those shoes." Luc looked wistful, remembering. "Maman said one day I'd have shoes like that – she thought everyone in Paris wore them all the time – maybe she wasn't so wrong after all." He looked at Ezra, eyes wide with excitement.

"Can they have big buckles, silver ones?"

"Hold your horses, Luc."

"Any metal'd do, honestly, so long as it's not clogs. They don't half hurt if they don't fit, and I don't think there's a clog maker in all of Paris carving shoes for boys with half a foot."

"You may be right. Shoes, then, with buckles," Ezra said, smiling. "Even so, we might have to take a cab – you can be my guide."

Luc sat up. "A cab? With a horse and everything?" He swung his legs out of the bed.

"Wait, I should check your wound first. I'll need to double-bandage it, and we'll have to find a way to take the pressure off."

Luc wasn't listening. "Jean won't believe this!"

Ezra begged some lambswool and extra bandages from one of the ward nurses, and after checking Figaud's stitching still looked neat, and there was no bad smell or necrosis, he bound Luc's stump and tucked in the ends. He bought a pair of shoes with tarnished, tinplate buckles from a man who had lost his leg above the knee and paid him well, then took them back to Luc. They were far too big. "There needs to be as little pressure on the wound as possible, I'll stuff the space with more lambswool, see," Ezra said.

Luc's eyes were round. The shoes made a most satisfying sound as he clopped along the wooden floor of the hospital corridor.

"We'll find you a crutch. Lean on me for now."

Luc almost fell over in delight. "I believe I have died and am in heaven."

Ezra asked the gatekeeper to call them a cab for the Cirque-Olympique. That was the best place to start. As they set off, Luc was almost too excited to sit still. He stuck his head right out of the window and waved until Ezra begged him to calm down, saying they needed to keep a low profile. Meanwhile, Ezra's head was full of questions. What would he do when they arrived? Did he really believe every word Luc had told him? Ezra sank back into his seat and hoped against hope that Loveday would not put herself in any more danger. He looked out of the window as the city rushed past in a blur. He may as well hope that day was night.

The Cirque-Olympique was to the west of the city on a wide boulevard, the Rue Saint-Honoré. As they passed the fine buildings and public gardens, Ezra could see there were plenty of people living well on the revolution. Then there were the coffee shops, alive with ideas and debate, the Paris that Ezra had imagined. They all flew past.

The cab stopped outside the Cirque-Olympique, and Ezra helped Luc down. From the name he had expected more of an actual circus, like the one that pitched up in the fields beyond Sadler's Wells at Easter time. But this was more like the Hippodrome Loveday had taken him to once in St George's in the Borough, a brick building, a cross between a theatre and a barn. The front doors, the ones the audience used, were firmly closed, but he and Luc made their way around to the back, where a couple of small children walked a tightrope tied between posts a little way off the floor. Three spotted horses cropped the grass watched by a girl in a green and gold dress cut short above her ankles, and a little further off two burly men smoked clay pipes as a couple of tired but even bigger brown bears sat on a nearby patch of scruffy grass, scratching at their collars and searching each other's fur for fleas.

Luc saw the bears and hung back. "They can fell a man with a single blow!" he whispered.

Ezra didn't think these two bears were about to fell much, so he left Luc, walked up to the men and asked in his best French if either of them knew Loveday. He was met with silent glowers.

"Do you know a Madame Lascelles?" he tried instead. "Franconi? Maria Franconi?"

One of the men spat on the floor and looked at him with contempt. *"Non."*

Ezra was, on the whole, entirely happy with his lot. He was not the tallest, nor the strongest, and his skin colour set him apart – but this did not bother him. Today, however, in front of these men, who were as wide as they were high, he wished he was more imposing, somehow more awe-inspiring – a little more like Lieutenant Colonel Dumas, in fact. He tried to hold himself as tall as he could, like Dumas, as if he wasn't in the least bit scared of anyone.

He wasn't convinced by the men's taciturn response – he noticed that one of tightroping children had looked up at the mention of Madame Lascelles. These people knew, he was sure. They knew the names, and they probably knew where these people would be. He tried to see into the dark of the building, but it was impossible.

Ezra cleared his throat. "It is a matter of urgency, please. If you could simply tell me where she lives?" He inwardly cursed; it sounded like begging. "I mean no harm, none at all."

The men were smirking now and Ezra felt like an idiot. They wouldn't tell him anything. He couldn't give up, but with the two men's eyes on him he felt like he had no other choice – perhaps he could find someone else to talk to, another way altogether of trying to find Loveday.

He was about to turn to leave, frustrated and embarrassed, when Luc hobbled over to him, one eye most definitely on the bears. Ezra watched in surprise as Luc launched into a high-speed, unintelligible – to Ezra at least – stream of what he assumed must be Parisian slang. Luc looked tiny in front of these men, perhaps a quarter of their size, his dirty blond hair falling into his face. He made the men laugh – Ezra couldn't follow the joke, something about cheese, it sounded like, cheese and drunkards – but the men were in stitches, practically rolling around. The girl with the spotted horses and the tightrope walkers came over and began to listen: Luc told more jokes, and his little crowd were riveted.

He threw Ezra the briefest of looks; Ezra nodded, seeing the men's attention was firmly on the boy, and slipped inside the darkened theatre.

It took a while for his eyes to grow accustomed to the darkness and for Ezra to realize he was behind the stage. He could hear something, someone whistling out in the auditorium – wasn't it bad luck to do that in a theatre? He swore Loveday had told him some old tale about it. But this sounded like a folk song, a round, the same few notes over and over again. He fought his instinct to turn back – after all, Mahmoud could still be alive and Madame

Lascelles might be the only one to know the truth. Ezra pulled the edge of the curtain aside and looked around.

It was slightly less dark in the auditorium: a few candles were lit, and in their light Ezra could see the person whistling high up in the rows of raked wooden seats that banked all around the performance area. The space was more like an expanded operating theatre than anything else, even down to the sawdust on the floor.

He should show himself, he thought. There was nothing to be gained from sneaking around. He was about to step into the light when he heard something outside – something breaking, raised voices – a voice he knew. Loveday!

Ezra bolted out through the curtain and across the sawdust to the main entrance. The glass panel in the door was shattered. He pushed open the door and there she was, rapier in hand, backing a furious Madame Lascelles up against a wall.

Loveday saw him, but she kept the sword firmly pointed at Madame Lascelles.

"You are lying!" Ezra thought he'd never seen her so angry. "Maria has told me everything—"

Madame Lascelles almost growled, "If you harmed a—"

"I would never hurt her. I am loyal. You!" She spat the word. "You…" She looked over her shoulder at Ezra. "I owe you an apology, Ezra McAdam. I thought these people my friends. They have betrayed me." Her eyes were both sad and angry. "They have betrayed *us*."

Ezra frowned. "So Luc was right."

"Where is Mahmoud? Maria said she didn't know." Loveday's attention was back on Madame Lascelles.

"You think I would tell you? That boy is worth more than money."

"So he is alive!" cried Ezra.

Madame Lascelles smirked. "Go back to England or wherever it is you are from. You will never find him. If you persist I will pass your names to the militia and you will both find you have urgent appointments with the National Razor. "

"Don't threaten me." Loveday boiled with fury. "I was a fool to trust you! You will take us to him, right now."

Madame Lascelles looked at Ezra. "I think your friend has a sickness of the brain. She sees but does not understand. This is no longer your business. He is ours. Remember that and leave while you can."

Loveday smarted. "He is not a thing. He is our friend."

The old woman was dismissive. "Your faces are known. This city is not safe. If the militia do not get you, there are many cracks in the pavement through which small people can fall." She snorted at Loveday. "You wield a sword but will not kill. I can see that in your face."

"You underestimate her, *madame*," Ezra said. "You would not be the first. Now, where is he?"

"Tell us!" Loveday demanded, her foil grazing Madame Lascelles' throat.

Madame Lascelles' eyes flickered briefly over Loveday's shoulder, into the theatre, and suddenly Ezra remembered the whistling. The sound had stopped, and Ezra could feel a presence behind him; he wheeled round just in time to duck a swing from a broom handle. An old man, cap pulled down low, smiled a toothless grin and advanced on Loveday.

"Loveday!" Ezra shouted in warning.

He watched as the man raised his weapon again, but Loveday was quicker, she slashed at his shirt with her rapier and it fell open. Ezra wished he had something, anything, he could use as a weapon, but there was nothing. He snatched a handful of sawdust off the floor and flung it in the man's face. Ezra looked around as the man stepped back, spluttering, but Madame Lascelles was already fleeing the scene, surprisingly nimble for a woman of her age.

"She's gone! Ezra, come on!" Loveday gestured with her rapier, and the two of them hared after the old woman into the street. The sun was beginning to sink low in the sky, and the blossom in the Tuileries Garden drifted in the early evening breeze like snow, as if nothing out of the ordinary was happening at all.

"This way!" Loveday called.

Ezra followed. They turned the corner alongside the theatre. Then suddenly Loveday pulled up short and Ezra almost ran into her. There, in front of them, stood Madame Lascelles, collecting herself, smoothing down her skirts. On either side of her stood the heavies who'd been joking with Luc. They glared at Ezra. One spat a ball of tobacco onto the ground.

Madame Lascelles' smile was like a knife. "You have met my friends?"

As Ezra watched, one produced a silver knife from inside his jacket and turned it over in his hand. He looked as if it had been a long time since he had used it on somebody and he was keenly anticipating having the opportunity.

Ezra put a hand on Loveday's arm. "We have to go," he hissed. More people were coming out of the caravans, half dressed for the evening performance: some wore what looked like underwear; others in white-face Pierrot make-up yet wearing ordinary jackets and breeches. The sight was distinctly sinister and completely terrifying.

Ezra could see they were outnumbered several times over, and he scanned the crowd for Luc. Had they thrown him to the bears? He hoped to heaven the boy had slipped away.

"There's too many of them," Ezra said, trying not to sound desperate. Time seemed to have stopped, and for a long second he imagined the circus people closing in, and Loveday frozen into stone. He tugged her arm again, and the two of them turned tail, racing up the street away from the circus.

Madame Lascelles shouted after them, "*Malheureux enfants!* I'll have your heads!"

Up ahead, a cab was pulled over at the side of the road, as if waiting just for them. Ezra couldn't believe their luck.

The leather flap on the window drew back to reveal Luc, grinning at them. "Come on. *Montez!*" he cried, opening the door.

Ezra helped Loveday in and called out, "Driver! Fast as you can. Hôtel-Dieu."

"No!" said Loveday. "To the corner of the Rue des Petits-Champs and the Rue Saint-Honoré. Quickly!" She lowered her voice. "We have to find Maria, before Madame Lascelles gets back to her – she must know something."

The driver flicked his whip and the horse broke into

an almost-canter, east into the city, to the Pont Neuf. Ezra looked out of the window as the circus receded into the distance, then finally sat back in his seat, out of breath. Loveday was smiling at him.

"I am sorry," she said. "I should have believed you."

"It's all right." He would have liked to embrace her then, but he could feel Luc watching them.

"You're not going to start kissing, are you?" said the boy.

They both looked shocked. "No!" It came out as a chorus.

"Good." He waggled his boot. "Because I might need some help with this, doctor, and I couldn't be having it if you was going mushy on me."

Loveday snorted a giggle. "Believe me, Luc. I have never seen Ezra McAdam 'mushy'."

Ezra pretended to be affronted, but he couldn't be for long. He was happy. They had escaped. Mahmoud was alive, even if they had not yet found him, and Loveday, fuelled by indignation, was glowing, brave; like her old self again. She took the gun out of a fold in her dress and loaded it in her lap as the cab rocked over the cobbles.

She saw Luc watching in awe as she cocked the weapon and checked the barrel was true.

"It might be best if you went back to the hospital," she said to him. "We have work to do: difficult, dangerous work."

"She's right," Ezra agreed.

"No, you don't. I'm not going back inside when I only just got out," Luc said, leaning back in his seat. "And anyway, you might need me to haul your sorry selves out of trouble. Again."

*　*　*

The driver sped down the wide Rue Saint-Honoré. The shops that lined the street had clearly been grand once, but most were now boarded up, or empty, windows smashed. "You sure this is where you want to get off, monsieur?" said the cab driver, but Ezra insisted, and thanked him profusely.

They turned into a side street, and Ezra suddenly recognized the milliner's shop that Madame Lascelles had brought them to only yesterday.

Luc stood on tiptoe, trying to peer into the gloom beyond the boards nailed over the window.

"Are you sure this is the right place?" he asked Loveday, who was knocking on the door.

"Of course I am," she said. "Like I said, if Maria's anywhere it'll be here." She knocked again. "Maria!" she called urgently. "Maria, it's me – Loveday!"

There was no response. Loveday frowned and got to work on the lock.

"*Pas vrai!*" Luc exclaimed. "She can pick locks, too?"

"Loveday Finch," said Ezra, "is a girl of many talents."

It wasn't long before the door swung open, and the three of them stepped into the musty interior of the disused shop. Supplies and equipment littered the shelves and surfaces, even the floor. A few hats remained, their lace and flowers faded, layered with dust. Ostentatious, Ezra thought. No wonder Madame Lascelles had gone out of business – only the wealthy would have been able to afford things like these.

Loveday led them through a door at the back of the abandoned shop, and as Ezra's eyes adjusted to the darkness, he could see this place was not so abandoned after all. They had come into a back room, where there was a small table, a stove at the side, some cupboards – a serviceable little living area. A staircase to the left looked well-used too, the promise of bedrooms upstairs.

"Maria!" Loveday called. "Maria, are you there?"

As she started towards the stairs, Ezra noticed something on the table. A note? He picked it up.

"Loveday, I don't think she's here. And it looks like this is for you."

Loveday read it aloud. It was, to Ezra's surprise, in English.

"Dearest Loveday, it is with a heavy heart that I must confess I have told to you a lie. Please understand as you read this that you are my dear friend and I would never wish to hurt you, but you have seen how hard things have become here. We took your friend Mahmoud captive. Madame Lascelles and Carlo and I…"

Loveday had to stop for a moment. She looked utterly betrayed.

"He has been a prisoner for all this time, in the hope we could sell him to some Russian contact so that we could survive this hellish revolution. But now that Carlo is lost it seems pointless. Money will not bring him back. I look at the boy suffering and I no longer see hope. My family is gone and I am sending a child to his death? I cannot. I am leaving Paris. It will be hard but I will find work somewhere else, honest work.

*"The kidnap was always Madame Lascelles' idea, but
I know this does not excuse Carlo and me from what we
have done. We were desperate – we wanted to survive.
I only hope this letter will redeem me a little, and that
you will be able to save him. He is held prisoner in the
catacombs—"*

"The catacombs?" Ezra could feel hope beginning to rise
in his chest. "The same tunnels we used to escape from
the riot at the guillotine?"

But Loveday was miles away, staring at the letter. "I
trusted her," she said. "Her and Carlo."

"She said they had no choice," he said gently. "You saw
Madame Lascelles just now – perhaps she was threaten-
ing them."

"Perhaps," said Loveday. Some of the steel was
coming back into her eyes. "It doesn't matter. We know
where Mahmoud is. We can save him."

"Loveday, please! I must counsel caution. For once,
listen to me. If we are to find Mahmoud, we must regroup,
make plans. Madame Lascelles—"

Loveday gave a dismissive wave. "She is all bluster."

"No, she is not. If she holds Mahmoud for ransom, if
she knows his worth, then she is a woman who makes
plans too. If we fly at her, swords up, she will swat us
away. You know that."

Loveday bit her lip and turned away.

"This is not London. We are no longer on home
ground. We must tread carefully."

"*Hoi*, enough of this, *Anglais*!" Luc cut in. "What's
going on? Are we to stand around here all day? My foot

feels as if a thousand devils are inside my boot this very second, sticking me with red-hot needles."

Ezra felt a wave of guilt. "I will dress the wound again. I should never have brought you."

Loveday folded her arms. "We cannot wait a day longer. Mahmoud's down there all alone. He must be terrified!"

"We will have to. We will do this properly, Loveday," Ezra said. "And to do that we need to plan and prepare. You know that. It has been a long day. I have not eaten since breakfast, and we must rest, we will need all our energy."

Loveday sighed a long breath out, she looked at him and nodded. "You are right, Ezra. You usually are."

Ezra gave her a brief smile. "We will find Mahmoud. And we will get him out of there. And maybe Maria too."

Chapter Nine

The Hôtel-Dieu
Île de la Cité
Paris
26 March 1793

Ezra cranked the generator until the thrum of electricity from the influence machine shuddered and echoed off the white-tiled walls of the laboratory. Renaud had a new subject, a young woman – or all that was left of her. Her head, severed high up her neck, rested in a shallow dish. If the afternoon light had not been so strong, and if the cut that took her head from her body had not been so livid and fresh, one might almost have thought she was still alive. When Ezra mentioned a bruise on her forehead, Renaud explained that she had been at the Conciergerie, the huge city prison that looked like a castle, all turrets and grey stone, for a month before her death.

"A prison, naturally, is a place of violence," Renaud said, not looking up from his work. "But no doubt, given her sentence, she could only have expected pain."

"I don't think anyone deserves—" Ezra began.

"We are building a new country, a new world," Renaud snapped. "If the people are not for us, then they are against us, and that is the end of it."

Ezra was silent. He was for the ideals of the revolution in every way. Liberty, equality, fraternity – they were ideas that made his heart sing. But for all he knew, this prisoner's only crime might simply have been a lack of total conviction.

He looked at the girl, or rather the head of the girl; her eyebrows and eyelashes were dark, her lips were almost maroon. There was a ribbon, dark green, grimy but still satiny, tying her hair away from her face. Ezra blinked and looked away. This was not a job for a sentimentalist.

He did not want to be here. For all that a few days ago he'd told Loveday they needed to take their time, he wanted nothing more now than to be storming the catacombs of Paris to find Mahmoud. But what he'd said was true. They needed to stick to the plan. Clever Loveday and streetwise Luc were out today looking for clues, trying to find out where they needed to search – and Ezra was stuck here, enduring Renaud's experiments and small talk and passion for severed heads.

"Bichat tells me you have found some quiet lodgings that were, no doubt, market gardens less than a year ago." The young French surgeon continued working while he spoke, attaching two wires at the girl's temples. "You should look in the cellar for potatoes! Out there in the sticks those new places are thrown up so quickly."

"It's just beyond Saint-Sulpice, hardly a walk from here."

"The Left Bank? Friend Bichat is of the old school – I remember him telling me he never crossed the river unless he had no choice in the matter."

"I see. Yes, well, it suits us," said Ezra shortly. It was true; having their own lodgings made it much easier to go about their plans.

"Miss Finch is with you? You should have brought her to see this. I believe I am almost there. So close to discovering how the life force may be ... well, not resurrected –" he laughed – "I cannot claim that, of course, but at least discovering the source of life."

"Indeed," said Ezra, trying not to look as uncertain as he felt. If Renaud's research really bore fruit, wouldn't it all be worth it?

Ezra forced himself to watch as Renaud turned the head carefully and attached the other wires to the severed muscles in what was left of her neck. He told himself he would not think about who she was, who she'd been. Renaud was right, these experiments were at the edge of knowledge, and wasn't that where Ezra, too, had always wanted to be? Perhaps, he told himself, there would be ways of operating in the future without pain, isolating completely the parts of the brain that felt the knife. Wouldn't that step make this young girl's last contribution to science a good thing?

"More power, McAdam!" Renaud called. "I do believe this subject is the one."

Ezra cranked harder. The machine grew louder, the girl's eyelids twitched, her lips began to curl. He had seen this experiment now nine, ten times; he should be immune to the shock of it, but somehow he was not. Renaud's experiments were no different – and what did they signify more than that the spark of electricity could produce movement?

"Lise!" Renaud shouted at the head, his face close to hers. "Lise Arnaud, hear me! Blink twice if you hear me! Lise, blink!"

Ezra saw the girl's eyes open, and for a fraction of a second there seemed to be something there, some sentience that spoke to Ezra of great fear, as if the electricity had dragged the being, the soul of this poor girl, back from eternal sleep and into the husk of a flesh and bone skull, in a bowl in a laboratory.

The girl's jaw dropped open. Renaud put his ear so close she might be whispering secrets to him. Ezra saw her eyes roll back.

"We need more power. That is the key to it, I am certain; with more power the vitality that had previously existed can be replicated, don't you see?" Renaud disconnected the wires that pinched the skin at her temples and at her neck.

Ezra took a deep breath. "I'm not so sure," he said. "I'm not convinced of the merit of these experiments."

There was a look of surprise, then a flash of anger on Renaud's face. "I know I will discover things that will throw open the doors of human knowledge. My theories do not stop here, with these experiments – not at all. Imagine if we were able to experiment on these unfortunates before their deaths as well as afterwards!"

"You mean, question them, interrogate them?" Ezra said.

"No, man! Experiment! See how the brain acts in life as well as in death."

Renaud waved Ezra over to another head, this one a man's, shaven on the top to reveal a patch from which a disc of bone had been removed, twice the size of a guinea.

Underneath, the brain was soft and grey, like cloth.

"See? It can be done in life, too – it just needs a smaller hole, I think."

"Trepanning? Making a hole in the skull while the patient is *alive*?"

"There was a surgeon here in Paris – de la Touche – who was quite enamoured of the procedure."

"For no other reason than to make his name. It cured nothing! It's pure quackery!" Ezra was indignant, this was circus medicine. "The ancients thought it cured headaches – if it didn't kill you."

"The prisons are full to bursting with souls as good as dead anyway. Don't you see? That's the beauty of it. I may as well use them as specimens before their heads leave their bodies. Save the National Razor from getting blunt." Renaud chuckled.

Ezra felt a little sick. This was against all his principles. He would dissect cadavers, *had* dissected them, with and without the consent of the person that corpse had once been. But operating on the living? To cause pain for no reason – that was torture, pure and simple. Ezra felt his blood boiling. He tried as best he could to keep his voice level.

"What you propose, sir, is nothing less than—"

There was a loud knock at the door to the laboratory. Renaud flicked him an annoyed look, and Ezra was more than glad to call a halt to the conversation and answer it himself.

It was one of the boys who ran errands for the gatekeepers.

"You were left this, citizen," he puffed, holding out a

note. Ezra thanked him and stepped out of the laboratory
– partly so the boy would not see in, but also to put some
distance between Renaud and himself. He turned the
note over. Loveday's writing, hurried and blurred where
the unblotted ink had smudged.

> *Come at once to the Church of St Michel. Do not waste*
> *one second.*
> *L*

Glad to take his leave of a still-simmering Renaud, Ezra
dashed out of the hospital gardens into the street and
hailed a cab. He promised himself he would never more
help that man with his inhuman work. He sat back in the
seat. Even making that decision lifted a weight off his
shoulders.

He reached the church a good thirty minutes later,
the entire journey lost in a wave of anxiety. Their plan
had been to watch Madame Lascelles carefully, at a distance, Luc's friend Jean employed at a decent rate to see
where she went and what she did. It hadn't taken too
long to find her entering the tunnels the same way he
and Loveday had exited them the day she'd dragged him
away from the riot at the execution; that was no surprise.
But they had not discovered exactly where she went once
the darkness had swallowed her up. Loveday had suggested using breadcrumbs until Ezra reminded her that
even if rats did not eat them, which they almost certainly
would, breadcrumbs would be entirely invisible in the
dark anyway.

What had happened? He prayed to the God of science

that Loveday had not gone down there alone.

Ezra stepped down from the cab and saw two scruffily dressed boys playing what could have been draughts on the flat top of a grave. A third leant against an upright stone scanning a row of shops across the road. They were rowing about the rules; he could hear them from the street. The one making the most noise and waving his crutch around was Luc. Ezra despaired. So much for discretion, he thought.

"*Hoi!* Luc, not only will the whole world hear you, but you are putting pressure on your foot!"

"Keep your wig on, American," Luc said. "I was having a discussion with Mademoiselle Finch about winning."

Mademoiselle Finch? Ezra realized too late that the second boy was no boy at all. Loveday grinned at him from beneath a boy's cap. "I never lose, I have told him," she said.

The third boy was Jean, and he at least looked contrite. "I told them to stop messing around. I said they'll be out of there any minute." Jean looked again towards the row of shops.

"*They?*" Ezra said.

"Madame L and some *gars*. She went in the coffee house with him. They've been there this half-hour at least. I followed them all the way from the Palais-Royal," he added proudly.

Loveday ducked down behind a gravestone and motioned for everyone to do the same. Ezra could not help but notice the grave was that of a girl called Rose Gachet, aged seventeen.

"There! She's coming out," Luc hissed.

"And see the cove she's with?" Loveday whispered.

Ezra chanced a look. There was Madame Lascelles, dressed in a plain brown woollen gown with a shawl tucked round her shoulders, pinned close, and carrying a basket. With her was a man, youngish, clean-shaven, hair cut in the most modern classical style; he wore a shiny, tasselled, small sword.

"He's no *Français*," Jean said. "I heard him talk."

As Madame Lascelles and her guest crossed the road towards the tunnel entrance, Ezra could see his clothes were of the highest quality – and distinctly un-Parisian. It could have been the high-cut jacket, or the fancy cape. Ezra looked at Loveday.

"That sword is Russian," she hissed. "I reckon he is too."

Ezra's heart sank. He nodded. It had been Russians who had kidnapped Mahmoud in the first place, in an attempt to destabilize the Ottoman Empire. Mahmoud had had a very different upbringing than an Ottoman prince might have expected to, thanks to the interference of his grandmother, the valide sultan; she had smuggled him abroad so that he could go to school rather than living a life of solitude confined in the palace. But the consequence of his education being a secret was that he had no protection against the enemies of the Empire.

"That's it," Loveday said. "We're going in right now. We have to. Mahmoud needs us."

Ezra watched as Madame Lascelles opened the iron gate and went inside, ushering the man in ahead of her. He made a face, smiled stiffly; no doubt the prospect of a trip into the tunnels under Paris was not entirely welcome.

"Come on." Loveday picked up her rapier and pulled Ezra along behind her.

"You're sure we won't get lost?"

Loveday showed him a bobbin of thread and gave Luc the end.

"It is not perfect but it is all we have. Whatever you do," she told Luc, "don't let go."

"You have my word. I will hold it tight and sit cross-legged on the road like a lame beggar."

"You *are* a lame beggar," Jean said with a grin.

Luc ignored him, settling by the entrance to the grave-yard. "I won't move."

"I'll make sure he doesn't," Jean put in. Luc gave him a look.

"We don't have time for this," said Loveday. "Hurry, we will lose her."

"Like Ariadne in the Labyrinth," Ezra said.

Loveday frowned. "Ari-what? Is that Greek? Bet he didn't have this." She opened her jacket, and Ezra could just see the dull gleam of the silver-handled pistol in the inside pocket. "Cocked and ready to fire."

"A very modern Ariadne then," Ezra whispered. "She was in a story. Ancient Greek. Mr McAdam swore by the Classics." He pushed the gates open as quietly as possible.

Loveday followed, putting a finger to her lips, and they both listened for the sound of Madame Lascelles' footsteps. They could still just about make them out, and they followed the old woman and her companion into the dark tunnel. Very soon the soft velvety blackness had swallowed them up. Loveday reached for his hand, and Ezra squeezed hers tight, but he took more comfort knowing that her other hand was holding the thread that would lead them out again.

The ground sloped quite sharply downwards, and Ezra was aware that the further they walked, the cooler it became. Loveday had her rapier out and held it in front of her; Ezra could hear the whisper of metal against earth.

They walked on, saying nothing. He didn't realize he was holding his breath until Loveday squeezed his hand and whispered, "There! Up ahead."

In the distance was the tiniest sliver of yellow flickering light. It looked as if it were far ahead and up, the size of a speck of dust. The ground sloped upwards again as they headed towards it, and the light grew from a speck to a slit. The slit widened momentarily, and the two of them hung back and watched the shape of Madame Lascelles lift what looked like a blanket rigged up as a door over another tunnel so she and the man could go through.

As they came closer, the thin light revealed the walls glistening with damp; here and there the tunnel was shored up with wooden piling. From behind the blanket came voices, two of them – one most definitely a man's, his French subtly accented.

Ezra put a finger to his lips and they listened.

"This is the boy?" the man said. He did not sound impressed.

"He came from London, Monsieur Boyarkov."

"My name is *Count* Boyarkov," came the sneering reply. "In Russia we do not believe in any of this madness that does away with kings."

"Of course, Count Boyarkov. We are certain, sir, he is of the Ottoman royal family."

"He looks as if you scraped him off the street. You expect me to hand over hard cash for this?"

"I am not a commodity!"

Ezra heard the familiar, imperious voice of Mahmoud, sultan-in-waiting, and could not help smiling. The boy was alive, and he sounded exactly as he always did, even speaking French. Life in captivity had clearly not sapped his spirit.

"The English girl told the truth," said Madame Lascelles. "He is the Sultan's son. She was returning him to his family. Did you not hear his voice? That's not the speech of a street boy.

"Well," Boyarkov answered, "his wit is certainly sharp, and his teeth look good. His hands, too, under that dirt, are not working hands. I think that I, on behalf of my country …" he paused, coughed, "I think we can take this boy off your hands."

Ezra and Loveday strained to listen. There was the sound of Madame Lascelles counting cash.

"Dix, vingt, trente… Attends." She did not sound happy. "This is not the agreed amount. You are off by a third."

"I have no more. Take it or take nothing."

Madame Lascelles sighed. The seconds seemed to stretch out, and in the low light Ezra noticed Loveday lift the gun, ever so slowly and quietly, out of her jacket.

"So you will take it. Good." That was Boyarkov.

Mahmoud shouted, "I'm never going anywhere with you, you son of a dog!"

"You will do as you're told, you Ottoman pig,"

Boyarkov laughed. Mahmoud swore, and suddenly there was the sound of splintering wood.

Loveday looked at Ezra in the half-light. "Now!" she whispered. Ezra grabbed hold of the blanket, and in one swift move tugged it hard away.

The scene that met their eyes was like one of the engravings Ezra often saw in the print shops around St Paul's in London, the ones that depicted hell. There at last was Mahmoud, hair wild and matted, face smeared with smuts and filth, hands bound in front of him. He looked thin but as determined as ever. A table had been turned over and broken; Madame Lascelles' face was a study of fury as she scrabbled in the dirt for the coins that she'd dropped in her surprise. The Russian scowled.

Ezra saw that Mahmoud's prison was a space cut into the rock, a kind of circular chamber with candles throwing a hard yellow light onto the hewn walls. High above was some kind of skylight, giving a different, softer, bluer light. Up against the wall stood a small bed – how long had Mahmoud been kept here, in the half-dark, in the dirt, worse than an animal?

But the Ottoman prince did not have the look of a victim. "You took your time," he declared.

"Who are these children?" Boyarkov demanded, turning to Madame Lascelles.

"Loveday Finch." Madame Lascelles shot a sharp, hard look at her. "What is this? Where is Maria? That worthless child must have told you—"

But Loveday was pointing the gun at Boyarkov. "Put your hands up!" she ordered.

Boyarkov smirked at her. "Stupid girl." With one

smooth movement he drew his sword.

Loveday cocked the pistol.

"You'll not fire." The Russian was dismissive.

"Stand up!" Loveday ordered. "Both of you! Stand against the wall, now." Her voice wavered, but Ezra knew Loveday, and he knew what made her tremble was anger and betrayal. He did not doubt that she would fire.

Madame Lascelles stood, but only after gathering up a few more coins. Boyarkov held out his sword, keeping Loveday at arm's length.

"Put your sword down," she said.

Slowly, quietly, Ezra crouched at Mahmoud's side, took a knife from his pocket and cut the rope that bound the boy's wrists. There were wounds where the twine had dug into his flesh.

Loveday flicked a look at Mahmoud, Ezra could see her anger rising.

The gun shook in her hand, and at that moment Boyarkov swiftly and deftly disarmed her. The gun skittered across the floor and Ezra scrabbled after it as Boyarkov advanced on Loveday.

Madame Lascelles pulled Mahmoud up roughly. "Come on, Turk boy. And you, Count Whatever Your Name Is, take him, go on."

Mahmoud bit her – hard. She screamed.

Ezra stood, gun in hand. He could see Loveday now had her rapier out, but Boyarkov would cut her down. He looked for all the world as if he was having a day out in the park.

"Three years in the St Petersburg Military Academy." He smiled. "The finest in the world."

Loveday parried, once, twice, forced the Russian back.

"A lifetime in the fencing school of life!" she said valiantly.

"You are a child," Boyarkov scoffed. "You cannot win." And with a couple of strokes Loveday was on the back foot, a cut all down one cheek.

She touched the blood, lost concentration for a moment. Ezra saw Boyarkov step towards her, smug triumph glinting in his eyes.

Ezra pointed the gun at the man's heart. No, he told himself, the head would be quicker... He hesitated. He was about to take a life. In that split second Madame Lascelles launched herself at him, and in a panic he squeezed the trigger. There was a flash of light and the small underground space was suddenly filled with an explosion of noise.

Everything happened at once. The rush of air guttered the candles into darkness and Ezra's ears rang with the sound. He lay on his back, the gun in his hand, his heart thumping like a horse galloping down a cobbled street.

He'd missed.

He must have hit the ceiling. Earth was falling in a fine rain, a fog of dust that entered his mouth, his eyes, and made him splutter and gag – the sound of his own breathing was distorted, and he couldn't hear anything else.

Ezra felt a hand grasp his, and for a second he froze. But he realized with relief it was Mahmoud; the hand was small, and he could feel the welts on his wrist. Ezra squeezed and held on tight, and together they stumbled forwards. They had to find Loveday. What had happened to her and Boyarkov? Ezra yelled into the darkness. "Loveday!"

Suddenly a face loomed out of the dust – Madame Lascelles, shouting something that Ezra couldn't make out as she hit out at Mahmoud with a chair leg, but Mahmoud ducked. Ezra grasped the chair leg. The old woman's grip was surprisingly powerful – it took all of his strength to wrest it out of her hands. Her face contorted in fury as she spat curses Ezra couldn't hear. He shoved the chair leg hard at her midsection, and she doubled over, reeling back into the dark.

"Loveday!" he shouted again, his own voice still sounding muffled to his ringing ears. "Loveday! Mahmoud!"

He squinted frantically into the dark, willing his eyes to accustom themselves to the blackness. He'd lost track of Mahmoud. He had to find him, find Loveday and her thread, or they were all done for.

He stumbled forward and all of a sudden he was standing on something soft and yielding, rather than the firm hard earth of the tunnel. Something human. There was an almighty yell, which Ezra realized must have been colossally loud, though he could barely hear it, and Boyarkov stood up and threw him over. Ezra felt his shoulder jar as he hit the ground. In the dim light he saw the Russian standing over him, saw the soft glint as he lifted his sword. Ezra felt for the gun – it was no use, he'd had no chance to reload. He kicked out, hoping to knock the man down. His foot collided with Boyarkov's knee and the man's face became a mask of anger. Ezra watched the blade descend and he twisted away.

Nothing happened. Ezra had expected the sharp sting

of the blade. He looked; the man was suddenly on the ground, blood arcing out of a wound in his neck, a dull grey fountain. He watched as the man pulled himself up and fell back again, saw the whites of his eyes.

Loveday wiped her sword, and put her hand out to help Ezra up. Ezra tucked the gun into his pocket and stood. She had Mahmoud behind her, and the three of them stumbled into the corridor.

"Madame Lascelles?" he spluttered. The air was still thick with dust.

Loveday was fumbling in her jacket pocket for the thread. "Mahmoud got her with the carafe."

"You do not know how long I have been waiting to do that," said Mahmoud grimly.

"Oh, Mahmoud," said Loveday, "I can't believe we have found you – at last!" She put her arm through his, and Ezra could just about make out her teeth in the darkness as she grinned and held up the bobbin of thread with her other hand. "Now, let's get out of here!" she said.

Ezra smiled with relief, and together they followed the thread up and out of the tunnel as fast as they could.

Chapter Ten

Rue des Lauriers
Near Saint-Sulpice
Paris
29 March 1793

Ezra came in from the tailor's just in time to see Luc slap down his cards on the rickety table in front of the fire and glare at Mahmoud.

Loveday shook her head. "If he asks to play cards with you, make sure you do not."

Mahmoud smiled with quiet satisfaction. "I was a champion at reversis at school in London. It was quite diverting."

"For you, *peut-être*!" Luc scowled at him. "You'd make a fortune on the streets with a pack of cards."

"Glad to see you are all making yourselves at home," Ezra said. "And far enough away from the Hôtel-Dieu that I don't have to invite Renaud for supper." He looked at Loveday. "I think the fellow might have a crush on you. He goes on and on about your visit. So I lied and told you had left for Italy already."

Loveday sighed. "I wish that we had. Although you never did describe his work."

"You would not believe me if I tried." Ezra put the bundle of clothes down on the table.

"Have you bought up all the goods in all the shops in the Palais-Royal, American?"

"Travelling clothes for us," Ezra said. "And a new pair of trousers for Citizen Luc."

Luc's eyes popped. He had never in his life owned a pair of trousers that had not been worn by someone else first.

Loveday swooped down on what was very obviously a new green dress. "I wish to wear this now," she said, standing. "They made all the pockets I requested?"

Ezra nodded. "Yes, indeed. And I have found you and Mahmoud space in the diligence for Le Havre. It leaves tomorrow morning at eight o'clock from the Place de Grève!" he shouted after Loveday, who was already on her way upstairs to put on the dress.

Luc looked forlorn. "Tomorrow? And you, American? You'll leave too?"

"I will, Luc. I have a business to attend to, and a living to make." Ezra did not add that he missed London more than he had imagined he would, the familiar streets and the comforts of his own home. Josiah and Mrs Boscaven. Nor did he mention that he welcomed the chance to get as far away as possible from Renaud and his unnerving experiments. "I have been away longer than I intended."

Luc turned away towards the fire. "You should take your clothes with you then. I will not need them." Ezra could hear the catch in his voice. "I cannot make a living as a cripple in new trousers! Jean said you would abandon me, and he was right. On the street it's all for one, but none of you care what will happen to me!"

He pushed himself off his chair and went upstairs too.

"Luc!" Ezra called after him. "Luc, I brought you something else!" He took the buns out of his pocket.

There was the sound of a door slamming upstairs.

"He is upset," Mahmoud said, unfolding his new jacket. "He does not want any of us to leave. But he is sulking, also, as I thrashed him at every game all afternoon." Mahmoud shrugged his old jacket off, put on the new coat and nodded. "This is acceptable," he said. "Although not as good as the one my grandmother presented me with on my eighth birthday. I think it was Persian. It had the most wonderful birds embroidered all over it, every colour one can imagine, the finest silk…"

Ezra smiled to himself. He would have liked to remind the boy that he had not long ago emerged from weeks underground wearing rags.

Ezra filled the kettle and put it on the fire for tea as Loveday came down in the new dress. She was smiling. "See," she said. "This is the new fashion – less fabric, and made in the Classical style. The Greek Republic comes to modern France." She sashayed around the table. "But with plenty of pockets."

"Good. I have enough money for your journey." Ezra lowered his voice. "There is no merit in trying to sell the ruby here; it will simply draw unwanted attention. Who knows if the Russians will send someone else after Mahmoud."

Mahmoud patted down his coat. "When we arrive in Venice my grandmother's agents will find us. Of that

I have no doubt. We will reimburse you, Ezra McAdam. Every penny."

Ezra smiled. "I owe you, both of you. I would not have my inheritance without you. I would have nothing."

"True," Loveday said. "You would be that naval saw-bones, walking the wooden world as cannon and shot blast all around you!"

Ezra looked uncomfortable at the thought. "I have had quite enough of war."

"And I have had my fill of Paris." Loveday sank into a chair by the fire and looked at the flames. "If my father were alive he would never have believed it. I cannot wait for the morning. To be on the road out of here." She sighed, heavily.

"I am sure you will not have to wait long for a boat at Le Havre," Ezra assured her.

"And when we arrive in Constantinople, my grand-mother will make certain you are most welcome," Mahmoud added.

"I don't doubt it," Ezra said. "I wish I could meet her myself. She sounds like a formidable woman."

"I assure you, Ezra McAdam, my grandmother makes your politicians look like babies. She may be a woman, but she knows how to get around anything that comes in the way of her plans. And Loveday, she will buy you a thousand dresses, or anything else you might desire."

"I hear –" Loveday grinned – "that Turkish steel makes for excellent foils."

Mahmoud shrugged. "Weapons if you prefer."

"And a tour of the palace?" Loveday asked innocently.

"That might be harder." Mahmoud made a face. "You

are, after all, a girl and an infidel."

Ezra smiled as he listened, and turned out his pockets – there were a couple of pamphlets that had been pressed on him outside the tailor's – and put on his new clothes too. He set out the buns on the table, and, having no plates, used the pamphlets instead.

"Loveday, will you fetch Luc? He is still cross with me."

"You can't blame the boy. Honestly, how's he ever to make a living?"

"That boy has more than enough wit. As long as he stays clear of reversis and other such card games he might do well," Mahmoud said. "He tells so many anecdotes and jokes. Did he tell you the one about the archbishop and the pineapple? Most entertaining, I thought."

"Tell him they have currants," Ezra said as Loveday picked up her skirts and went upstairs to find him.

As Ezra arranged the buns, he found his eye drawn to one of the pamphlets. There had been a failed coup, apparently, one faction of the army attempting to seize power from the revolutionary government, but the men of the American Regiment had stood firm. Ezra smiled. He did not doubt it. Dumas was the best soldier and the most principled man he had met in his short time in France. Yet the article went on to disparage him:

Colonel Dumas – who it should be remembered is a marquis in name, though his skin is as dark as any mulatto's – has the impudence to visit the War Office in person to request more resources for his American Regiment when it is a fact known to every man, woman and child in Paris that the Americans merely have to click their fingers and the wealth of the Americas would be available to them. For shame, Colonel Dumas!

Ezra felt rising fury on behalf of Lieutenant Colonel Dumas. The man should be celebrated, if only for that day in the rye field. He should get a medal, not have his reputation trashed by shoddy pamphleteers. He crumpled the paper up and threw it onto the fire and watched it burn.

"I despair of this country sometimes," Ezra murmured. "They run around like headless chickens." He stopped himself, he did not want to be reminded of Renaud and his ghastly experiments.

"Yes, well," Mahmoud said, reaching for a bun. "If a people *will* throw off their ordained ruler…"

"Oh, for pity's sake!" Ezra was not going to have an argument with a sultan's son about the rights of man.

"I am in the right. I have experience of how a ruling family can—"

Ezra stood up. "Let's have no more of this, please. I am of the opinion that all men are equal. You and Luc, myself and Loveday…"

"Loveday, I grant you, is an exception."

"There. We are all exceptions."

"And Luc? Does he not deserve more than a life on the streets?"

"Of course!"

"Yet you, Mr Citizen Surgeon, act as if his future is of no account to you. You change his life then cast him out."

"I didn't—"

146

"Then you will sleep safe and sound in your well-appointed – if rather poky – town house in Great Windmill Street, will you not, while Luc is abandoned, a poor half-foot boy on the streets of Paris?"

"No!" Ezra retorted indignantly.

"So you will do something?"

Loveday chose that moment to come back downstairs, followed by Luc, who was clearly not sulking so much that he could not be brought around by the promise of currant buns.

"Ah, Luc!" Mahmoud smiled. "Ezra has brought buns and has some excellent news."

"I have?"

"Yes, as you were just telling me, you feel that poor Luc needs a patron, shall we say, and with this in mind you have resolved to take him back to London and enrol him in your small but nevertheless reasonably comfortable household." Ezra opened his mouth to protest, but Mahmoud took no notice. "Light duties only, of course," he added.

Luc gaped at Mahmoud, and then at Ezra. "*Vraiment?* You would really hire me? But I – I cannot leave Paris behind, it is all I know."

"There, you see," Ezra began, but Mahmoud waved a hand dismissively.

"London is not so different from Paris," he said. "And anyway, you will not need to know the streets there – you will be fed and clothed and have a roof over your head."

Luc stared at Ezra with eyes like plates. Then his face lit up, and he hobbled across the room to fling his arms around Ezra's neck. "Oh, American! I shall be so grateful, you will see! I will not hate the English and I will work as hard as any boy with only half a foot has ever worked."

"No, I..." Ezra looked from Mahmoud, who had an unflappably smug look on his face, to Loveday, who was surprised but clearly amused. Luc gazed up at him like a puppy that only a lout of the lowest quality might kick out of their way into the gutter.

"The deal," Mahmoud said, taking a sip of his tea, "is sealed."

Ezra could not in good conscience argue with him.

The rest of the afternoon was passed in more games of reversis – which Mahmoud continued to win – and quadrille, which Mahmoud said was the best game for four players. But the rules were so long and drawn out that Luc fell asleep by the fire before they could start.

It was early evening when Loveday, wrapped in her new cloak and carrying her second-best sword, went out for some cheese for supper. The dairy was just round the corner, where the main road into the city crossed their little row of new houses. Ezra watched the door close behind her, and thought how much he'd miss her; she and Mahmoud would take weeks to reach Venice and then on to Constantinople. Ezra told himself that none of the destinations plotted along the rest of their course would be as chaotic as Paris, but he couldn't help wondering. Once she and Mahmoud took their seats on the diligence tomorrow, would he ever see her again? And if she *did* finish her journey safely, would he simply receive another letter in a few months' time saying she was staying with old friends of her father's, in Italy or Germany or somewhere else across the Continent, the better to try her luck plying her trade there?

Ezra sighed. He sat back by the fire to think, but Luc yawned awake and looked round, blinking.

"Was that Mademoiselle Loveday leaving? Did she remember, I wanted some buttermilk if there was any."

Ezra got up and put on his coat. "I'll catch her up." They had spent very little time on their own; the walk back from the dairy might be their last chance for a while.

Outside, the sun was setting. A lamplighter moved along the street and the city shone pink and gold. It was, Ezra thought, as beautiful a city as London. And like any city, it didn't do to look too closely at the dirt and it was always best to shut your nostrils to the smell. He looked ahead and saw Loveday's green skirts turn the corner into the main road. The street was still busy, people hurrying home from work. Carts and barrows trundled westwards. Ezra quickened his step.

As he neared the crossroads he noticed people scurrying out of the way as a knot of National Guardsmen marched by. Ezra counted seven or eight of them, in a variety of worn and dusty navy coats with tricolour rosettes pinned on their caps. They looked more like a street gang than military men – drink-worn rather than battle-hardened, scrutinizing the civilians with suspicious eyes.

The troop marched past the crossroads, and the onlookers visibly relaxed as they passed.

Ezra hesitated. Should he speed up or slow down, warn Loveday to stay out of their way? No – she would be in the dairy by now, he told himself. He would hurry down to the corner and watch as the militia marched away, and

Loveday would laugh at him for being scared.

He turned the corner and stopped suddenly. Shouts and crashes could be heard from inside the dairy, and nearby shopkeepers were running to see what had happened. Ezra pushed his way through, and felt his heart tighten in his chest.

Loveday stood facing down four militia men, rapier drawn; behind her, ashen-faced, stood the dairyman's boy, a youth of fifteen with a half-grown brown moustache.

"He is innocent!" she was insisting. "He doesn't deserve the guillotine!"

"Out of the way, *mademoiselle*," barked the commander. "This boy is an enemy of the revolution. He was seen throwing turds at members of the Revolutionary Council. He is an agitator and a spy."

"For shame!" a woman shouted. "He is Laurent, the dairyman's son. He waters the milk, but…"

The commander glared at her intensely. "Perhaps you would like to tell us more as you accompany us to the dungeons at the Conciergerie, Madame Citizen?"

As the commander turned away, Loveday darted forwards, rapier at the ready. The other officers surged forward to hold her back and wrestled the sword away from her, but not before she'd caught the commander a sharp slash across the cheek. His face became red with incredulous fury – although not as red as the blood trickling from the cut.

"He's no spy!" Loveday spat. "Just a boy who's probably sick of watching people get hauled off to prison for no reason!"

The commander struck her hard across the face. "What

is your name, girl?" Ezra felt his heart pound. He was rooted to the spot. Surely Loveday would at least have the sense to give a false name?

"Loveday Finch," she snapped defiantly, and the man's eyes narrowed.

"Finch? That's an English name," he growled. "She is a spy – this young man is clearly in league with the English! Take them away." The officer who had Loveday by the arms began to haul her out of the dairy, and the dairyman's son was shoved after them.

Ezra tried to push his way towards her. Loveday looked dazed, her face red where she'd been slapped, but then she caught sight of him and shook her head and mouthed something: *Mahmoud*. She stared hard at him then, and Ezra knew she meant that he should be the priority – without either of them, Mahmoud would have little hope of ever returning safely to Constantinople. He felt sick to his stomach as he watched Loveday and the boy, Laurent, being marched away down the street. She was right – of course she was right – but Ezra wished to heaven he had the gun.

He ran back as fast as he could to the house. Luc was drinking tea and playing patience. Mahmoud was packing a small bag. He froze when he saw Ezra's face.

"It's Loveday," Ezra said. "They've taken her to the Conciergerie."

Chapter Eleven

Ezra crossed the Seine on the Pont Saint-Michel at a run, his heart hammering in his chest. He had left Mahmoud with Luc, and loaded the gun and slipped it into his new coat pocket. He had tried to hail a cab into town all along the Rue de Sèvres, but none had stopped for him. Now, he thought, he was too close to bother. The lamps were lit all along the bridge and the shops that lined both sides blazed with yellow candle- and oil-light. Street singers and hot-chestnut sellers, acrobats and pamphleteers blocked his way as he dodged and ran through the crowd, his legs slipping and stumbling over the cobbles.

Ezra could feel the sweat running down the back of his neck and into his clothes.

Up ahead against the darkening sky, the Conciergerie loomed on the north bank of the Île de la Cité. It reminded him of a more severe sister of the Tower of London, hunched against the grey, pond-still Seine. He still felt in shock; one moment all had been well, he had finally felt as if things could turn out all right – and now that sense of relief had been torn from under him as abruptly as tendon from bone. What was his plan? What would he do? Could he persuade them to release her? He thought about how dismissive the commander had been, and his heart sank. Loveday had attacked a member of the militia. They would never willingly let her go.

He stopped, panting, at the main entrance. There was a guardhouse with a full complement of militia in the same mismatched coats and cockaded caps. There was a small crowd, too – a few men, but mostly women, children at their skirts – begging the guard to take parcels of food, flagons of wine, beer, to their husbands, wives, sisters, brothers... Babies cried, and children, bored, kicked stones and played leapfrog.

Every one had a story as tragic as the other. Mahmoud had been entirely right. Ezra would gain nothing from rushing up to the most heavily fortified prison in the city with a pistol and an angry heart. He had to use his brain. That was, as Mr McAdam had always told him, the best weapon of all – although Loveday never believed it. He studied the lists of new prisoners that were posted outside the gate. If Loveday was to have a trial it would take a few days, maybe even a week, before she came to court. There was nothing he could do but wait. Some went straight to the guillotine without a trial, but he could not allow himself to dwell on that; he *would* not.

Ezra tore himself away from the foreboding sight of the prison, trying not to let despair clutch too tightly at his heart. He looked up at the skies: through the smoke of the city there was a half-moon and a few twinkling stars. He hoped she could see them. He hoped she was not too cold.

As he walked back towards the bridge, Ezra passed the huge building of the Hôtel-Dieu. Renaud, no doubt, would still be hard at work listening to dead people gargle out their thoughts. He stopped. Renaud – the Conciergerie! Hadn't he wanted live subjects from the prison for his experiments? Ezra glanced back over his shoulder towards the bleak, hulking shape of the Conciergerie. Perhaps he could use Renaud's obsession to his advantage.

Ezra altered his course and made for the hospital gates. He might have vowed never to work with Renaud again, but surely there could be no better reason to break a promise than to save a life.

The gatekeeper was eating some kind of sausage, small pink gobbets of which flew from his mouth as he told Ezra that Renaud had already left for the day. Ezra cursed under his breath. Would he have to wait until morning?

"At this hour you'll find him in the coffee house off the Cœur du Palais – if that's what it's still called nowadays," the old man went on. He spat a piece of sausage onto the ground. "I forget."

Ezra offered his effusive thanks and the old man garbled a long list of directions.

"It's behind the Palais de Justice. If you cross a bridge you've gone too far."

So Ezra made his way back into the medieval heart of the city. The Île de la Cité was crisscrossed with tiny yards and alleys, buildings seeming to curve up and over the street. Lamps were strung on ropes that hung between

154

top windows. Shop boys swept ashes and trimmings and all sorts away from doorways and into the gutters.

Surprisingly, Ezra found the Palais de Justice quite easily. In fact he realized he must have passed it earlier on his way to the prison. He wondered if that was where they'd take Loveday when she went to trial. It looked big enough to rival the Old Bailey. He cut through an alley and found himself in a small courtyard. He looked around to get his bearings and saw the bright yellow light of a coffee shop. There, framed in one of the small squares of swirling window glass, nursing a mug and reading a pamphlet, sat Renaud, snug in a black top coat, his hat beside him on the table.

Ezra went in, making the bell on the door rattle, a high thin sound over the hum of chatter. Inside, the air swam with the fug of smoke and the tang of tobacco. Renaud looked up and smiled.

"McAdam! This is a pleasant surprise. *Mon ami* – I had thought you'd left town. I must say the coffee here is a thousand times better than the stuff Bichat makes." He waved Ezra over. "Sit, I'll order you coffee. I have something to tell you."

Ezra sat and took off his hat, turned it over in his lap. Renaud called to a waitress and she brought them over a fresh pot of coffee and a cup for Ezra.

"I must speak with you." Ezra tried not to sound too desperate. He lowered his voice. "About your work…"

"I am ahead of you, man!" Renaud took a flask of something from inside his jacket and tipped it into Ezra's coffee before he could protest. It smelt like rum. "The best spirit. Straight off the boat from Saint-Domingue!"

Renaud leant close, scanning the coffee shop as if he believed all the souls in the place were hanging on his every word. "I have the letter from the governor." Ezra looked at him, uncomprehending. "The governor of the Conciergerie! My name will go down in history. Every honour will be mine!"

Ezra picked up the coffee cup. The man was odious and self-regarding.

"Congratulations. You will be receiving some, er –" Ezra paused; what was the correct terminology? – "live subjects, fresh from prison, then?"

"Ah. Sadly no. The governor is not convinced that his reprobates and counter-revolutionaries will not escape."

Ezra almost choked.

"Are you quite well?"

Ezra coughed hard and Renaud thumped him on his back.

"Rum too strong for you?"

It took Ezra a few moments to compose himself.

"No. Not at all," he said at last. "I was merely surprised. You seemed so sure, about your work."

"Indeed I am."

"But your subjects?"

"That's it, dear friend. If I cannot bring the prisoners here, I will set up my clinic in the Conciergerie itself. The governor has allowed me into the prison – I will conduct my experiments in trepanning and isolating parts of the brain in the infirmary. There is so little light. Tiny windows." Renaud shrugged. "But it can't be helped. Science will prevail. I will discover the secrets of human consciousness." He grasped Ezra's hand in his excitement. "Since you are still here – and I hope for the next week at least? – might you accompany me the day after tomorrow? As my assistant, of course."

Ezra put down his coffee cup. He nodded. He hoped his voice didn't give his feelings away. "Of course." He couldn't bear the thought of the man's experiments, but if it could get him into the prison, perhaps he could find Loveday, somehow spirit her out.

Renaud bid him come to the Hôtel-Dieu tomorrow to help prepare for the trip to the Conciergerie, and Ezra reluctantly agreed. Keeping himself occupied would, at least, help to keep his mind off Loveday's fate.

The walk back through the dark city streets matched Ezra's mood. By the time he reached the house in the Rue des Lauriers he had told himself that if he was to rescue Loveday himself he would need help – and Mahmoud and Luc did not count. They were a couple of children; his responsibility, not his seconds.

A door opened and a woman threw the contents of a chamberpot out into the street. Ezra only just dodged the stream of filth in time. He pulled his jacket closer – the frost was setting in – and hurried on. He had never felt so alone in all his life.

The house was quiet. Mahmoud had fallen asleep by the fire, the still-glowing embers lighting the room a soft pale orange. Ezra found a blanket and covered him. The young prince murmured and stretched in his sleep, like a cat, then snuggled down into it. His face was a picture of peace – no troubles touched him.

Ezra put a new log on the fire and set about cleaning the table. It had been left just as it was when Ezra had followed Loveday out earlier: the crumbs, the pamphlets. Hadn't there been one about Lieutenant Colonel Dumas? Ezra looked for it before he remembered that he'd burnt it on the fire. He told himself he should try to get some sleep himself; he would need to think clearly if he was to get Loveday out of this.

He sat at the table and took the gun out, turned its silver handle over and over, then set it down beside a pamphlet that promised freedom and liberty for all men – even slaves and women. Ezra managed a wry smile, though he felt sick to his stomach. Would that it were true.

He turned the pamphlet over, but the reverse merely bore the words of a new revolutionary song. He should go to bed. Ezra felt a heavy tiredness in every bone of his body, even as his mind raced. He got up, scraping the chair across the stone floor, and Mahmoud sat up, suddenly awake.

"Loveday?" the boy said, rubbing his eyes.

Ezra shook his head.

"I didn't think they'd let you in. I mean, you hardly look like any kind of professional," Mahmoud said. "Too young and far too dark-skinned. No doubt they imagined you as some kind of agitator. If these people had any kind of proper respect for sovereigns I would simply accompany you. As it is, no doubt they would have my head as well as hers."

"Loveday is still alive," Ezra snapped. "And will remain so if I have anything to do with it!"

"There is no need to vent your fury on me, Ezra McAdam! I assure you, if we were closer to home I would but snap my fingers – or at least persuade my grandmother to snap hers – and Miss Finch would be at liberty!"

His tone was imperious as always, but Ezra could tell the prince was genuinely distressed beneath it all. Ezra sighed in frustration and sat back down. "We are not in Constantinople, Mahmoud."

Mahmoud sighed. "You promise you will save her?"

Ezra nodded. "I will do everything I can to get her out of there. But you and Luc must be on your way. I cannot think about saving Loveday while I am worrying about you as well. You will take the diligence tomorrow as arranged, and Luc will accompany you in Loveday's place – his wound is healing, and he has said there is no pain. The two of you should find somewhere to stay in Le Havre, and Loveday and I will catch up with you, when we can."

Mahmoud frowned. Ezra could imagine his protests – Luc was savvy enough on the streets of Paris, but he, too, was only a child, and he only spoke French; he would be a poor substitute for Loveday. But, Ezra thought, Mahmoud needed *someone* to accompany him, and perhaps his straight-backed imperiousness and Luc's irrepressible cheek might balance each other out. At least until they reached Le Havre. At least until he and Loveday could catch them up, and then she and Mahmoud would journey on to Constantinople and Ezra would take Luc back to London, as he had promised. He felt a sick panic rise inside him whenever he dwelt on Loveday's future plans for too long.

"You may be sultan one day, but for now I am in charge," said Ezra before Mahmoud could speak. "You will do as you are told."

Mahmoud thought for a moment, then nodded.

"Good," said Ezra. "I have to go to the Hôtel-Dieu tomorrow and work with that devil Renaud. I am hoping he will help us, one way or another."

"You and Loveday *will* follow?" Mahmoud asked, and for once he sounded like the young boy he really was.

Ezra did not look him in the eye. "Of course."

The morning broke crisp and sunlit, the city veiled in a sparkling sugar coating of frost that transformed the dirty grey buildings into what Ezra imagined a magical kingdom might look like. Roofs and towers glistened, the air so sharp and cold that every smell of decay and taint seemed to have been cleaned away. Even the old turds in the street were frosted and shining. The back streets, though not paved with gold, shone like silver.

The three of them walked into the city in silence – even Mahmoud had lost some of his swagger. When they reached the Pont au Change Ezra did his best to lift their spirits.

"I –" Ezra paused, corrected himself – "I mean, we – that is, Loveday and I – will join you as soon as we can." As he spoke, Ezra straightened the lapels of Luc's jacket without thinking.

"I had wanted to bid Jean farewell," Luc said in a small, un-Luc-like voice. "He might think I have died. I must tell him!"

"There is not time," Ezra said, a little too forcefully, and Luc's face fell.

"What if you do not come?" Luc said.

Ezra coughed. "We will come." He turned Luc's face to look at him. "I have promised Mahmoud, and now I promise you."

"But we should have some other scheme in mind," Mahmoud added quickly. "Just in case."

Ezra nodded in agreement. "Just in case. Give us two weeks. Two weeks, then get on the first boat that sails to Venice."

Luc bit his lip. "I've never been on a boat. I knew a joke once about a boat but I've forgotten it. We will be all right, won't we, American?"

Ezra squeezed his shoulder. Mahmoud tried to smile.

"Mahmoud says you made Miss Finch disappear into thin air once, and if you can do that, getting her out of prison must be all in a day's work."

"Well," Ezra said, "I will do my best." He felt a lump in his throat the size of an apple. He coughed. It would not budge.

The pair of them seemed so young, so vulnerable. Suddenly he had an idea; he reached inside his jacket and took out the silver-handled pistol. He pressed it into Mahmoud's hand. "Take this," he said. "Keep it out of sight."

Mahmoud nodded, slow and courteous. "I am grateful, Ezra McAdam. The whole Empire is grateful."

There was already a crowd on the bridge, scurrying to and fro on their way to work to open shops, to sell vegetables, make gloves, slaughter animals. Ezra looked around and hoped that no one had noticed.

"You know how to use it?" he said, his voice low.

"I had a pair of my own once," Mahmoud answered. "More than one pair, in fact, though my favourite were the pearl-handled—"

"Your best bet is to keep your heads low. Don't say

anything stupid, not about things you own, or royalty, or politics."

"I am not an idiot," Mahmoud snapped.

"I'll keep him in line, American," Luc said.

Mahmoud arched his eyebrows, and Luc grinned. "We'll be all right."

Mahmoud hid the gun and put out his hand. Ezra shook it, then watched them as they disappeared into the crowd.

Ezra looked up at the Conciergerie across the river. Its grey walls appeared white and frosted and heavenly in the morning sun, and it seemed more like a palace, a child's drawing of a castle, than a dungeon.

He would see if Loveday's name was on the bills later, take her some food if he could.

Ezra took a deep breath and turned his step towards the Hôtel-Dieu with a heart so heavy it might have been made of cast iron.

Chapter Twelve

The Hôtel-Dieu
Île de la Cité
Paris
30 March 1793

"Ezra McAdam! I welcome you!" Renaud wiped a bloody knife on his leather apron and beckoned his English colleague inside the laboratory. The young man was grinning – no, worse than that; he was, Ezra thought, unbearably smug.

Renaud went on, "The season is not on the side of the anatomist, it may still be cold now, but spring is on its way and soon our specimens will decay as the summer sun warms all our bones, dead or alive!"

"The frost is still evident today," Ezra said, pleased to be able to have some kind of conversation that did not involve Renaud's experiments.

"But not for long," Renaud said. "I am hoping to impress on our director the practicality of building an ice house right here."

Ezra smiled as he tied on his own apron. He could not fault Renaud's reasoning; in fact he had looked into the possibility of building one at home. He studied the man.

Was he a kind of reflection of himself? So driven, so keen to discover?

Renaud fetched his instrument case, which was covered in fine black fish skin, and when he opened it Ezra saw it was lined with ruby red velvet. "It would extend the season, you see. Dissection would no longer be governed by the time of year. In London, no doubt you have a few more chilly weeks – here we may be throwing off our winter jackets before April is out!"

Ezra looked around. There were no heads today save one. Instead, in the centre of the room, there was an uncovered cadaver, mouth sewn shut, one arm dangling off the table as a man in sleep. Ezra went over and put it back by his side, adjusted the man's head and centred the porcelain neck rest. His instinct, borne of years of training, was to study the man, read as much information about the fellow as he could. What was his employment? Were there any signs of illness? The corpse had been a healthy-looking man who had worked outdoors by the colour on him, and some kind of physical work judging by his well-muscled shoulders, which displayed tattoos that indicated he had, at one time at least, been a sailor. He had a large shot wound in his stomach. The edges where the ball had entered were beginning to blacken and necrotize. Ezra frowned – this body was far from fresh.

"Don't worry about that," said Renaud, seeing Ezra's expression. "I need this cadaver here for a specific reason. The first thing we have to do is turn him over." Renaud bustled over. "My theory will be proven, and this is but a first step. Come, man, your help."

Together they turned the man face down.

"I want to lay bare the spinal cord first and then take the brain and the major nerves out intact. I want to see the pattern of nerves leading from the brain stem. It is my contention that the brain is the principal organ and seat of all life."

Renaud set out a variety of flesh knives and a bone saw ready for use.

"I will take off the cranium. If you would steady the specimen…"

Ezra assisted as Renaud began, and he had to admire his skill with knife and saw. He was not a butcher, he knew exactly what he was doing, each cut made with economy and care even though the subject was too dead to complain. As the young man worked, Ezra thought perhaps it would be better to lay his cards on the table – concerning Loveday, that was. He needn't tell the whole story about Mahmoud, simply that Loveday had been picked up by the guard and now languished in the Conciergerie, her fate uncertain.

"There was something…" Ezra began.

"Hmm?" Renaud looked up from where he was carefully laying out the nerves and artery systems like so many discoloured ropes.

Ezra took a deep breath. What had he to lose? "It's Miss Finch. Remember? Miss Loveday Finch."

"A most lively wit, and clever, I thought, for a young woman." Renaud picked up a heavier knife and began to separate the vertebrae. "Most engaging." He stopped, looked at Ezra. "You and she…? Were you, I mean, was there a, shall we say, understanding between you?"

Renaud was blushing. The man was definitely sweet on Loveday. He would want to help her, Ezra decided.

"Oh no!" he answered. "I assure you, there is nothing of the kind between us."

"I thought, well, you seemed so close and easy with each other." Renaud sighed, a knife smeared with flesh and body fluids in each hand. "I have always found it hard to talk to young ladies. I tell them about my work and suddenly they lose all interest." Renaud put the knives down and picked up the bone saw again. "Miss Finch seemed so –" he paused – "so different."

Ezra smiled. "Miss Finch is different, yes. I met her last year in London; her father had died, and then my master. We became close, but as siblings, as brother and sister. Nothing more."

A brief smile passed over Renaud's face, and he began cutting through the cranium. The sound of bone resisting metal echoed off the tiled laboratory walls.

He stopped a moment. "But Miss Finch is already en route to Italy, you said. This last week." He looked back to the cadaver and then at Ezra again, anxious. "Has something happened to her?"

"Renaud, I must admit to you that although she was supposed to leave Paris, she hadn't."

"What?" Renaud waved his saw at Ezra.

"Yes. Something has happened." Ezra swallowed. "I'm afraid I lied about Italy – well, not completely. She was to embark for Venice as soon as—"

"Spit it out, man!"

"She got into a row with the militia yesterday. Defending a boy in a dairy."

"And?"

"Now she is in prison, in the Conciergerie. She hasn't

gone to trial, but I know how impatient Miss Finch can be with authority. I was hoping since you plan to make a visit to the prison and take me with you…"

Renaud was still working at the cadaver, its head hardly attached, the vertebrae exposed, but now he looked up again, pushing the hair away from his face to stare at Ezra. "My God!" he gasped. "What are you asking?"

"There must be a way to get her out."

"Yes. Wait for the trial, and when she is cleared—"

"You think that's possible? She is English, they will know that by now. And she used her sword on the soldier, even if with little consequence – Loveday speaks with her sword. She is heading straight for the guillotine!" As Ezra voiced his worst fears, he knew, with a sickening sense of inevitability, that this was true.

Renaud was pale. "But I cannot. I could lose my position. The support for my work."

"Loveday! She will surely die. We could save her. *You* could save her."

"How? Feign her death? Help her escape?"

Ezra felt hugely relieved. "Yes! Exactly."

Renaud threw the saw down and the metal clanged around the room loud and discordant enough that it could have woken even the half-dissected man on the table. Ezra realized he had pushed too far. Renaud was tugging off his leather apron. "I will pretend this conversation never happened. I understand you are upset. Indeed, I am too. Miss Finch was –" his voice was choked, he coughed – "a rare specimen. If you wish to work with me you will not mention her again. And as to accompanying me to the Conciergerie tomorrow – I think not."

Ezra bridled. "But she needs our help, man. *Your* help. It's in your power to free her."

"Smuggle her out, you mean? Out of the most heavily fortified prison in Paris, in all France?" He paused. "Do you have any idea what you are asking?" Renaud was shaking with fury now. "To put my life and my work in jeopardy? Miss Finch is an enemy of the people. They will have justice!"

"Loveday is only the enemy of bullies and cowards! She has done nothing to warrant her own death, and neither have at least half the men or women locked up in that place!"

"You would do better to hold your tongue!" Renaud glared at him, and Ezra wished he'd been more temperate, less impassioned.

Renaud hung up his apron. "If you want to be of help, finish up here. I must get some air. I will not speak of Miss Finch or have her name mentioned ever again. Is that clear?"

He slammed out of the laboratory, leaving Ezra to pick up the bone saw from the floor. He swallowed, wiped the dirt off it, then resumed sawing, carefully, slowly, until the top hemisphere of the skull came off in one neat piece like a poorly made wooden fruit bowl. He set it down on the table. The cadaver's brain was grey and jelly-like. It was truly, he thought, a most mysterious organ.

Ezra sighed, deep and heavy, as he fetched a porcelain bowl large enough for the brain and brain stem and calculated the amount of preserving fluid necessary to cover the organ completely. What in heaven's name had he done? Hoped that Renaud would be somehow swayed by his emotion into a heroic action that would imperil his own life? Of course not. He should have known the man was far too dedicated to his science.

Ezra hesitated. He was about to take the large bottle of preserving fluid off the shelf when it occurred to him that he might be better off leaving the Hôtel-Dieu as soon as possible. It would be no surprise if Renaud returned with a company of guards to lock him up, too. He looked at the cadaver on the table, no longer a man: a body, a torso and limbs. He would make it tidy, then leave, stop by to see if there was a trial date set for Loveday, then clear out the house at the Rue des Lauriers. He would buy another gun, some ammunition, and perhaps intercept Loveday on the way to her death – they may both go down together, but at least he would have tried. He imagined Loveday's response to his plan. Brave and stupid, not like Ezra McAdam at all.

He tidied the cadaver as best as he could and took off his apron; he was about to leave, quickly and quietly, when the boy from the morgue came careering round the door of the laboratory.

"Sir, Citizen Renaud! I know I should have knocked, sir, but this is an emergency!"

The boy pulled up short.

"Renaud is not here," Ezra told him.

The boy was breathless. "You are a surgeon? You must come in his place."

"But—"

"One of the Revolutionary Council has come in. Citizens Bichat and Figaud are out of town – please, he is dying, you must come to the theatre at once!"

Ezra snatched up the apron he'd just taken off, picked up his instrument case and followed the boy, who sprinted across the courtyard and through the doors into the theatre.

Ezra could hear the screams of agony from outside. When he arrived in the half-empty theatre he saw a man, his jacket off, his white shirt red with blood, being held down by two of the hospital porters.

Ezra saw the man's face, and in spite of his wild hair and dishevelled, blood-stained clothing, he knew him – it was General Le Brun from the War Office, calling down curses on every man, woman and their dog in Paris. Ezra could only guess at the specifics; even after all the time he'd spent with Luc, he could make out only a little of the foul language that came gushing from Le Brun's lips, at a volume that might wake the heavens.

When the officer saw Ezra, the look on his face registered such fury that it had the effect of stopping him dead in his tracks.

"Is there no one else?" Le Brun screamed.

"You are welcome to wait, citizen, but you are bleeding." Ezra was calm. "And I would suggest that the sooner we staunch the flow, the better."

"You will finish me off!"

"I will not. Now, if you would remove your shirt, sir." Ezra knew all patients to be in this heightened state. He took in the venom in the man's face and corrected himself. "Citizen."

"These brutes have me pinned down. What do you suggest?"

Ezra nodded and the porters let him go. Le Brun peeled away his shirt. It was sodden, and as the fabric came away

170

Ezra could see the man was bleeding copiously.

"I am dying!" Le Brun yelled. "I will not have this man touch me!" he shouted at the porters.

"Calm yourself," Ezra said. "Do you wish to lose more blood? I am the senior surgeon here right now, and unless you wish to be cut apart by students, you will let me look closely. What happened to you?"

"That devil Dumas! I challenged him to a duel – he would not accept the end of his regiment."

Ezra swallowed. He must keep his feelings in check. He looked at the wound, the cut went all across the man's torso from the shoulder, the skin flapping open like yet another layer of fabric, but this one living, bleeding. It was cleanly done, grazing his ribcage and finishing at his stomach. Ezra relaxed.

"I do believe this looks a deal worse than it really is."

"That bastard meant me death."

"I assure you that whoever did this did not mean to kill. I have seen duelling injuries before – a hair's breadth more, yes, and your internal organs might be damaged. But this blood, citizen – sir – is mostly show. Now, it would not do to lose any more of it, so please, keep still and I will repair you."

Le Brun was shaking. "You lie! You are in league with the devil who did this to me! He did not finish me off, so you will!"

"Citizen Le Brun, I am in league with nobody. Now, although this wound is superficial, any more blood loss may cause serious harm." Ezra kept his voice cool and level as the porters held Le Brun down.

The general passed out after Ezra had put the first few

stitches in. The French sutures – the finest cat gut by the look of it – were high quality, but Ezra remembered the master's words and only used a few of them, attempting to encourage the flap of skin to close instead with the effect of tight bandaging.

Renaud came into the theatre just as Ezra was finishing swaddling Le Brun. He commended Ezra's needlework, leaning close enough that Ezra could smell the drink on him.

"I am sorry, Renaud," he said. "What passed between us earlier—"

"Not here," Renaud snapped. He changed his tone as Le Brun's eyelids fluttered awake. "Some brandy, citizen?"

"Do any of you know who I am?" Le Brun struggled to sit up, and winced.

"Do not exert yourself, please, I beg you." Ezra said. "Those stitches…"

"Am I a divan, that you would upholster me? Have you stuffed me with horsehair?"

McAdam here has done his best." Renaud shot a look at Ezra. "Come, Citizen Le Brun."

"I would take a cab home this instant!"

"I do believe a carriage ride would be best undertaken after some healing," Renaud said. "Please, we have a room for you away from the wards."

Ezra raised an eyebrow but said nothing. So much for equality, he thought.

Renaud indicated to the porters, who helped Le Brun off the table and led him away.

Ezra wiped down his needle and took off his apron. He

inspected his new jacket: Le Brun had bled most copiously and there was some staining on the shoulder. New clothes were wasted in this job.

A boy of around Luc's age cleaned away the worst of the bloody sawdust.

"Good work, citizen sir," the boy said, sneaking a glance at Ezra as he swept.

Ezra tossed him a coin for his trouble.

"One day," Ezra said, "you will be me."

The boy beamed.

Ezra stepped out into the spring sunshine and regretted it immediately as there, across the courtyard, Renaud was bearing down on him, face like thunder. He took Ezra by the shoulder and virtually pulled him along and towards laboratory.

"We must talk," he said curtly.

"I will not turn myself in," Ezra insisted. "Call the guard if you wish. I will try and free her on my own if you will not."

"Not here!" Renaud hissed.

He pushed Ezra ahead of him into the laboratory and closed the door behind them, sliding the bolt shut.

"I have decided," Renaud said, his hair flopping down into his face.

Ezra could not have been more surprised if the fellow had hit him around the face. Renaud paced up and down, twisting his hands over and over as he did.

"I said I have decided. Mademoiselle Finch deserves my help. I have made my decision." He paused, and Ezra said nothing for a while. Was he hearing correctly?

"What say you, McAdam? I thought about Miss Finch

all morning. Your request first struck me as impertinent, outrageous, beyond the law of the land. But then I realized that my work into the seat of consciousness, the work I want to do on the human brain, is beyond most ordinary people's understanding too."

Ezra nodded. "I should say that it is."

"There! You have it. My work is exceptional, as is Miss Finch! We shall spirit her out of the Conciergerie and she shall live."

Chapter Thirteen

The Conciergerie Prison
Île de la Cité
Paris
31 March 1793

"**C**itizens! The governor is expecting me – er – us."
Renaud tried to sound firm but Ezra could hear the tremor
in his voice. They had loaded up a cart with the main parts
of Renaud's influence machine and now waited outside
the gate to be allowed into the prison. The horse flicked
its ears, the crowd murmured. One child squeezed to the
front, a smaller boy clinging to her side, and reached up
to tug at Ezra's trouser leg.

"*Maman* is inside, please tell her Paul and me are safe
and well. She is a seamstress, Anne Duchamp, from Les
Halles! Tell her, *je vous en prie*!"

The boy did not look well at all. His lips were cracked
and there were dark circles around his eyes. The cart
moved forward through the gates and Ezra swallowed.
There were, no doubt, hundreds of folk inside these
thick grey walls who deserved freedom. He turned away,
squeezing his hands into fists as they trundled through
the heavy wooden gates. He was determined to keep his

resolve. He and Renaud had discussed the plan long into the evening by the front window inside the coffee shop near the Palais du Justice. It was as simple as possible: today they would map the castle and look for Loveday; then tomorrow they would smuggle her out under pretence of some dire and most fatal infectious disease that could only be treated in isolation in the Hôtel-Dieu.

Ezra looked across at Renaud. His face was alabaster white and his knuckles gripped the cart hard, as if his life depended on it. Ezra might not have held much fondness for the man, but he had to give him his due – he was clearly terrified, and yet he persisted.

"McAdam!" Renaud hissed. "We are in."

A boy ran up to the cart and took the reins, and Renaud called down to him, "We need a couple of strong arms to unload. And tell the governor that Surgeon Citizen Renaud is here!"

They now stood in the prison courtyard. All around, sheer stone walls rose up above them, studded with a thousand tiny barred windows. There was the unmistakable stench of human filth and misery. The great wooden doors closed behind them with a dull, heavy thud, and suddenly the sounds of the city, of the crowd beyond the door, had vanished. There was only the soft murmuring of sobbing, punctuated by the occasional, hopeless cry from somewhere in the prison. The working men, laundry women, porters that went about their work, were curiously quiet. Ezra fought the urge to shudder. They would free Loveday, whatever it took; he must believe it, as must Renaud.

Ezra nodded to Renaud, trying to seem more certain

for the other man's sake at least. Renaud's lips were almost blue; it was as if the temperature inside the prison courtyard, even with the fire of rubbish burning yellow against one of the walls, was a few degrees cooler than the rest of the city. If there was a hell, Ezra thought, they had driven into its very heart.

They were shown up to the sick bay by the governor himself – a well-fed man, clean-shaven, pressing a rather expensive-looking silk handkerchief over his nose to keep out the stench – together with a warder holding the largest bunch of keys Ezra had ever seen. Some were old and rusted, a few were new and cast in shiny metal; most were at least four inches long. The weight of them seemed to drag on the fellow, they clanked and rattled as he walked. Even the door to the sick bay took three of the things, and the wait seemed interminable while he unlocked first one dead-lock and then another.

Ezra had seen the paupers' wards of the Hôtel-Dieu and thought he would be prepared for a prison sickroom. He was not. Inside, the straw on the floor ran free with vermin and every surface seemed coated in a greasy black layer of dirt, even the sheets. There was a fire in the grate, and set close to it stood a pair of high-backed wooden chairs with padded arms, where two heavy-set and barely shaven men sat, one reading a newspaper, the other cutting his toenails with what looked like a bread knife. An old woman with a scarf wrapped around her neck – at least, Ezra thought she was old, but she may have been merely thin and unwashed – stood in the corner leaning on a broom. The prisoners, who were kept at least three to a bed, seemed so close to death that Ezra had seen corpses healthier. In the short walk through the ward, Ezra saw signs of starvation, several varieties of pox, and poor souls with more ulceration than skin.

The governor kept the handkerchief over his nose and mouth as they walked through, and Ezra saw Renaud retch. The smell in the air was practically solid, of blood and pus and faeces and urine and necrosis.

Ezra helped the porters unload the equipment into a small room off the main sick bay. Renaud threw open the window and stood as close to it as possible. Ezra joined him, trying to breathe down as much fresh air as he could. From here Ezra could see the cathedral, and behind it a line of iron-grey clouds. If he looked down there was the gleaming silver ribbon of the river, and a throng of boats hurrying to and fro. It was a comfort to know that outside, the world was going on as usual. He made a silent wish that Mahmoud and Luc would be close to arriving at Le Havre and safety.

Ezra looked round at the smaller room as Renaud reluctantly left the window and began to fuss over the influence machine. The room was just big enough to set it up and squeeze in a couple of wooden chairs with straps and a small dissection table. Everything was as filthy as in the sick bay. Ezra drew a line with his finger in the black grime on the windowsill and made a face. Renaud saw him, and looked for a moment as if he might be sick.

"Citizen Renaud, are you…?" the governor began.

"I am quite well," Renaud said, standing upright again. "If you could possibly provide someone to clean—"

"Oh, but we scrubbed the room out only last night."

The governor hadn't taken the handkerchief away from his mouth and had to repeat himself more loudly. Renaud's face fell, but apparently the matter was settled as far as the governor was concerned. He went on, "I will accompany you to the cells. Shall we say an hour to ready your equipment?" Renaud nodded and tried his best to smile as the man in charge left.

It was a relief when they were alone, but Renaud exploded as soon as the door had closed behind him. "How in heaven's name am I to work like this? Every surface is alive with all the biting and jumping creatures that plague man." He brushed at his arms and legs and cursed. "And you expect me to risk my life in a pretence! I have half a mind to call the whole thing off."

Ezra was suddenly afraid. "But…"

Renaud waved a hand. "I am just saying. Fear not. I will go through with this trial." He sighed. "Miss Finch…"

"You will ask for her – well, not by name," Ezra said. "Ask for a red-headed girl."

"I know that!" Renaud snapped. Ezra wished he had more confidence in the fellow.

Renaud hurriedly pulled a small metal flask from his jacket pocket and took a long gulp; smacked his lips. "That's better," he said. He stood up, dabbing his mouth.

There was a loud moan from the sick bay and Ezra hurried through to find a prisoner in the throes of death. He snatched back the sheet, heavy with dirt, and found the pour soul's legs a mass of infected ulcers. He was suddenly furious. Not simply with the revolution, which should never have conspired to lock up Loveday – or Anne Duchamp of Les Halles, wherever she was, or any of these poor wretches who were closer to death than to overthrowing French liberty – or with Renaud, who was obviously pickled, but with everything. What was the point of all his training as a surgeon if he couldn't do a thing to help these living corpses?

Ezra called to the warders, "Fetch a copper of water and set it on the fire to heat!" The old man might not live long, but if it was up to Ezra he would die clean. "And let's have some light in here, and fresh air!" Ezra made his way down the line of windows, throwing open every one. But the warders paid him no attention until Ezra threatened them with Renaud's influence machine. He saw the woman with the broom smile. "Excuse me, *madame*," he said to her, "is there a linen store? Can you please find me some spare blankets?"

She nodded and hobbled away, turning her broom upside down and using it as a crutch.

Ezra rolled up his sleeves, gathered the worst of the filthy straw and set it to burn, sending flames leaping up the chimney and several mice and rats scurrying frantically for the darkest corners of the sick bay.

By the time the governor's man returned to take them down to the condemned cells to select their specimens, Renaud had his influence machine up, humming and fizzing, and the old man with the ulcerated legs had died, but the ward was cleaner. Those that lived, Ezra thought, looking round at his work, might survive a little longer.

The governor's man said that only Renaud was to accompany him to the cells, so Ezra took the chance to inspect the cadaver of the old man with the ulcers. Renaud had told him he was not to bring that foul corpse anywhere near his machinery, so Ezra moved it into the corridor. This was a chance to look at patterns of infection. Had the poisons in the wounds finished him off? Was the dirt in some way to blame?

Some of the man's ulcers were definitely healthier than others. Ezra peered closer. The healthier wounds all seemed at first glance to contain moving grains of rice. Ezra looked closer – these were maggots! This man had been incubating flies while still alive. Ezra looked again. They were actually feeding on the dead flesh, effectively cleaning the wounds. Was this possible?

He blinked. He knew how difficult it could be to cut away infected flesh. Might this be an idea? If the maggots ate only the diseased flesh and left the rest, this could be a way forward. For a moment he forgot about the prison and Renaud and the revolution, and it was as if he was back in London. Perhaps it would be hard to persuade some of his wealthier clients to incubate maggots, but if it could be shown to stop infection... Ezra was already imagining the experiments. Then he remembered that Loveday might never see home again, and his heart once more plummeted to his boots. He could only hope that Renaud would find her.

A couple of porters arrived to take the body away; they wound it in a sheet before he could take a closer look.

"Excuse me," he said, "where will you take the corpse?"

One porter smiled. "Friend of yours, is he?"

"No, I—"

"I know, I was joking," the porter guffawed. He and his partner lifted the body between them. "He's headed to the Hôtel-Dieu. Your friends there'll cut him up for fun, *non*?"

They carried the body away and Ezra was left in the corridor that overlooked the main courtyard. The bell of Notre-Dame thudded for eleven, and he could see Renaud out in the yard, making a selection from the chained and bound prisoners who were waiting to step into the cart that would take them to the guillotine. Ezra shivered. Would they face an even worse fate with Renaud and his influence machine?

He had to go through with this, he reminded himself. It would be worth it for Loveday.

While he waited for Renaud to return, Ezra kept himself busy in the sick bay. The old woman, he realized, was not quite as old as her stoop made her seem. She brought Ezra a cup of rather thin grey tea and whispered something so softly that he thought he had imagined it. Ezra looked at her. "Did you speak?"

The woman looked nervously towards the warders by the fire and put a finger to her lips.

She took Ezra by the hand and led him to the bed furthest away from the fire. There were only two patients in this bed and they were squeezed top to tail, one a toothless, hollow-cheeked, grey-haired old woman, the other a young girl, not yet twenty, Ezra thought, with thin yellow hair and skin so pale she could have been blue. She coughed a little, a terrible rattling sound that shook her whole body, and the woman on the broom suddenly seemed to melt, stooping to push the girl's hair away from her forehead.

"There, there, Juliette, *c'est Maman. Je suis ici.*" The

woman took the girl's hand and stroked it tenderly as she whispered to Ezra, "My Juliette is under sentence of death. I got work here to see her, to be with her. To try and protect her, but –" the woman paused; Juliette coughed some more and Ezra couldn't help but wince in sympathy – "I pray the illness will take her first."

She glanced towards the warders but they were engrossed in a game of dice. The woman looked desperate. "If you had something that could see her on her way…"

Ezra was stunned. A mother who wanted to kill her own child? He stepped back. "Madame, I—"

"Do not judge me. She is dying anyway, I am not a fool!" The old woman sighed. "She turned down a boy in the militia, and he fashioned a plot against her. All lies." She shrugged sadly. "It is old news. She became ill before she was sentenced."

Ezra felt for the girl's pulse; it was weak. She was dying, he could see that.

He looked out into the courtyard, there was no sign of Renaud.

"Madame…"

"My name is Durant. Marie Durant. Please, if you can help."

Hadn't Ezra wanted to do something? But … killing?

"Your –" he coughed, stepped away from the bed, kept his voice low – "Juliette, she will be dead soon, one, maybe two days. I don't see—"

Juliette opened her eyes. "Please." She looked at him, her eyes were milky blue. "My chest hurts so much." Ezra could see that every movement, every breath hurt.

Juliette coughed again, harder, deeper, shaking her whole body. The toothless woman at the other end of the bed clapped her gums together and turned over.

Ezra looked from Madame Durant to her daughter. He gave a brief nod and went to see if Renaud had brought any medicine with him. A heavy enough dose of laudanum would do, he thought, to send the girl into a sleep she wouldn't wake from. He checked himself. That would be murder, wouldn't it, as surely as if he struck her with a sword? He could hear her still coughing in the other room. Or was her mother right: was it a sort of kindness?

Ezra had Renaud's bag open when the other surgeon came back, and had just found a twist of paper with what looked like a few grains – not enough to kill her, but maybe to soothe her last few hours. He pocketed the twist and snapped the bag shut just in time. Behind Renaud, a warder led two men who were chained together.

Renaud commanded the men to wait outside. He was glowing, nervous. For a moment Ezra thought he'd done it, thought he'd somehow had a word in the right ear and Loveday would be freed.

"Loveday?" Ezra looked past his French colleague. He could only see the two men. "What happened?" he hissed.

"No women." Renaud shook his head. "We are not allowed to use women. The governor shouted at me when I suggested it, said I was a devil!"

Ezra was silent. Renaud closed the door behind him.

"I can't – this plan of yours, it won't work," Renaud hissed. "And what were you doing in my bag?"

"Nothing – well, no, actually, looking for laudanum to treat—"

"These prisoners? These scum? Don't waste your time! Come on, McAdam, we are ready to meet the future!"

Ezra felt a sudden wash of dismay. "Loveday is the only reason I am here!"

"McAdam, leave it! She is gone and that is that! We cannot."

"Cannot? No! We are here!" Ezra looked at Renaud. "Did you ever mean to help us?"

Renaud grabbed hold of Ezra by his lapels, put his face right up next to his. "This work is more important than anything," he snapped. "I will not let you or any girl get in the way!"

Ezra pushed Renaud off him. "You can do your 'work' on your own then, *sir*."

Ezra slammed out of the room, past Renaud's subjects and across the sick bay. He was so close to Loveday. To give up everything now! He saw the woman sweeping in the corridor.

"Citizen?" she begged. "Sir doctor…"

Ezra handed over the paper. "This will help her sleep at least."

Marie Durant was grateful. She wiped the tears from her face with her filthy apron and sniffed. "If there is anything I can do for you?" she asked, and Ezra realized she looked concerned – was his distress so clear? He tried to pull himself together, shook his head.

"No, no, I'm sorry, no." He began to move away, embarrassed. Then he had an idea. He turned back. "Madame

Durant, perhaps you *can* help me. Do you know these cells well? I need to find someone."

There *was* still something he could do.

Ezra peered out of the sick bay window to where Marie Durant had told him the women's wing stood, across the courtyard and to the right. On the top floors were the rooms for prisoners who could pay for their keep – these rooms were better than her lodgings, she'd said. The middling floors were where most women were kept, the ordinary sort who engaged in work to keep themselves busy and to earn their keep.

In the basements were kept the difficult prisoners. Madame Durant said there weren't many women who couldn't be kept in line with violence, or the threat of it at least. Ezra didn't say anything, but he imagined that was where Loveday would be.

No one stopped Ezra or asked what he was doing as he descended the stairs, and his confidence rose. He would find Loveday by himself; between them they would devise some way of walking out of this place, and be on the coach to Le Havre and freedom before the end of the day. Ezra reached the ground floor and looked out into the courtyard. Warders in one corner were shoeing a horse in front of an open forge, the sound of iron on iron echoing around the space, ringing out over the racket of the prisoners. Ezra took a deep breath and stepped out into the courtyard, walking as purposefully as he could towards the women's wing.

There was no one manning the outer door, so Ezra walked straight through, and once inside he took the stairs down to the basements. Now he could hear singing and moaning and yelling. The prison was like nothing so much as a menagerie for human beings. It was inhuman to lock people up, Ezra decided – as inhuman as keeping them five to a bed in a charitable hospital. If they weren't animalistic and violent already, they very possibly would be after a few nights in a place like this.

He turned a corner and found three warders huddled in a circle; they all looked up from their game of dice.

"What d'you want, citizen?"

For a second Ezra froze. He hadn't thought this far. What had he imagined? A corridor of locked doors? The chance to run along and shout her name? Would these men know her? Of course not.

He tried to stay calm, tried to summon up all the confidence he could. He remembered standing on the stage at the Ottoman Embassy in London wearing a magician's cape and hat, looking out over the audience and making Loveday disappear in the blink of an eye. He fixed the largest warder with a steely eye, thought of him as a medical student who did not know his vena cava from his aorta.

"I am looking for someone," he said as loudly and clearly as he could, trying not to sound too English.

The man looked him up and down. One of the others spat into the fire, making the hot coals sizzle.

"*Ici?* They're all trash of one kind or another, American. On whose authority?"

"The governor's," Ezra said firmly. "I am with Citizen Renaud of the Hôtel-Dieu."

"American!" A woman's voice called through the bars from a cell up the corridor.

Ezra's heart leapt for a moment, but it wasn't her – of course it wasn't. Would Loveday call him "American"?

"I'm not Austrian – I'm not even German and they lock me up!" She kicked at the cell door. "There's a girl in here sick. Dying. Is he a doctor?"

"Surgeon," Ezra replied.

"Sawbones!" she sneered. "What good is that to us? Can you cut away the fever with your knife? Lop off the pain where they whip us?"

Another voice called out from a nearer cell, "A doctor?"

"No!" the first woman answered. "He's a sawbones, he says."

"I can help!" Ezra said.

"Got any laudanum?" another woman shouted. There was laughter; desperate laughter.

Soon the corridor was alive with noise. The second warder stood up.

"See what you gone and done now?" he said to Ezra, then took in a lungful of air and yelled, "Quiet! You lot of cats can shut up or I'll let this fellow in myself and set him about to cut off any bits that're still making so much as a squeak!"

There was an outbreak of curses and groans, but quieter, and above the complaints there suddenly came a voice he knew. "McAdam?"

Ezra bolted down the corridor towards the sound. "Loveday!" He couldn't help shouting her name. "It's me!"

And he saw her, smiling, her short red hair standing up around her head in clumps. She was still wearing the new green dress, now torn and filthy. And even though there was blood dried around her mouth and dark circles the colour of soot around her eyes, a sorry sight, Ezra was grinning so wide that his face might have split in two. He reached out and grabbed her hand through the bars.

She looked at him. Were her eyes moist? Was Loveday Finch on the verge of tears? "I knew you would come," she said, her voice cracking, the sound only a step above a whisper.

Ezra turned to the warders. "My man, there has been a mistake. This prisoner—"

The women jeered and called. The largest warder strode towards Ezra, fingering his keys. In his mind's eye Ezra saw him unlocking the door. Ezra and Loveday would walk out of here yet.

"*Monsieur!* If you please," Ezra said.

"*Monsieur*, is it?" The warder let go of the keys and they fell against his leg, jangling. "Aren't we all *citizens*, American?"

"Yes, naturally. If you would just…"

"What did you call her?" The warder glared. "And what did you say you were doing down here anyway?"

One of the women in the cell pushed her way forward. "He called her Loveday. Loveday? What kind of name is that?"

"An English name." The warder made a show of looking thoughtful, and he picked up his keys again and unlocked the cell door.

Ezra was caught on the brink of victory. There was a flicker of anxiety behind Loveday's bravery. He tried to keep his own face steady.

The warder fought off the scrum of prisoners and plucked Loveday out, pulling her hard by the arm. Ezra could not help but notice the size of his hand, large and pink as a ham closed tight around Loveday's forearm. She flinched but kept her face stony.

"Loveday is it?" The warder put his face up close to Loveday's.

"You can let her go. Please," Ezra said. "She is my responsibility now."

"Oh, you misunderstand me, Citizen American. She is not going anywhere with you."

The second warder sneered. "If she's English she can go straight to your friend and associate the governor. If she's English she's most definitely a spy, and we know what happens to them, don't we?"

Loveday was trembling. Ezra began to feel desperate. "The governor would not want this."

"I don't believe you are any sort of a doctor at all," the warder growled. "Look at you. Not even a full-grown man, and the wrong colour for learning." He laughed. He was missing nearly all his teeth.

Ezra stood his ground. "I am here with Citizen Renaud, at the request of the governor himself."

"And I am King Louis the Sixteenth," sneered the warder.

"Let her go! Let her go now!" Ezra cried.

The man was already dragging Loveday back to the cell. She tried to pull away but there was no strength in her. Ezra had to do something. He threw himself between the warder and his friend and attempted to prise the man's hand off her forearm.

The warder batted him away as if he was no more than a moth. Ezra stumbled.

"I said let her go!"

"Shut your trap, you…"

Ezra didn't hear the rest. He saw the man's hefty pink fist coming at him and he stepped back, but not quickly enough. He heard the crack of bone – was that his own jaw? His nose? – and felt an explosion of pain in his face as the blow swept him off his feet and his body collided with the floor, which seemed to have rushed up to meet him at an alarming rate.

Chapter Fourteen

The Hôtel-Dieu
Île de la Cité
Paris
31 March 1793

Ezra spluttered awake, cold water stinging his face.

"You hot-headed idiot!" Renaud hissed. "I should have known. Your kind…"

Ezra remembered saying her name aloud – he had given her away. What a fool! He winced, and it wasn't just the pain in his jaw.

"Idiot!" Renaud repeated. "You have ruined everything. I am never working with you again. Ever. You're lucky the governor didn't lock you up."

Ezra tried to get up. Everything ached. He saw the windows above him and realized he was in the laboratory of the Hôtel-Dieu, lying on Renaud's dissection table. For a moment he imagined he was dead; this was a dream, and Renaud was about to crank up his influence machine. He tried to sit up again, but Renaud stopped him.

"You've had a blow to the head. Several, in fact. Don't worry, I wasn't about to drill a hole in your skull. Although the thought had crossed my mind."

"Where's Loveday? Where is she?" Ezra pushed himself up in spite of Renaud, and the room swam for a moment before settling into focus.

Renaud folded his arms. "Back at the Conciergerie. They decided to make her an appointment with the guillotine for tomorrow. Your appearance rather moved things along. The governor has rescinded permission for my experiments. They practically threw my valuable influence machine onto the cart with you – I fear they've damaged it. Boneheads! Donkeys! *Mon Dieu!* This is all your fault. I should never have let you talk me into your outlandish schemes. A girl!" Renaud laughed. "For a girl you would kill yourself – and not only that but bring the progress of medical science to a complete halt!" Renaud threw a metal bowl across the room in exasperation; the sound bounced and clanged around the white-tiled walls.

Ezra recalled seeing Loveday being dragged away by the warder as the world went black. He closed his eyes. "I thought…"

"Here's some advice. Don't think. You're clearly not very good at it." Renaud was shouting now. "Stop thinking and get out of Paris at once. I only saved your sorry skin because you are a brother surgeon."

"But Loveday!"

"What? What can we do now? There is no way we can help her. If you had not blown my experiments I might have been able to find another way."

"Experiment on her? I would never let you near—"

Renaud snorted. "What, you want to keep her for yourself?"

Ezra glared. "You and your experiments disgust me."

"Hypocrite! I knew it. Happy to slice our dead friends from stem to stern, but when it comes to real progress, real discoveries, you recoil. Your name will be lost to history for ever, whereas mine – you will see – will be carved in stone."

Ezra's ribs ached. He suspected he'd had a kicking from the warders before Renaud found him. He felt the swelling around his chin and moved his jaw sideways a little. It clicked painfully, but nothing was broken. He would live. He thought of Loveday, though, and felt sick. Tomorrow! Tomorrow she would die.

"Get out. Now." Renaud marched to the door and held it open. "I must have been an idiot to think we could free anyone from the Conciergerie. The foremost prison in the city – you must have infected me with madness!"

"Not madness," Ezra said, the words tumbling out of him. "Something else, something you will not have heard of. Loyalty, and friendship. If there is no one you would risk your life for, I would ask yourself if your existence is worth anything at all."

He picked up his medical case, the one with Mr McAdam's initials embossed in faded gold letters, and tried to walk out of the laboratory as steadily as he could.

He didn't look round as Renaud slammed the door.

Ezra made his way uneasily towards the hospital gates. He felt a little better for telling Renaud the truth, even if it made no difference to the man at all. Ezra nodded at the gatekeeper, and bade him a last goodbye. The gatekeeper smiled back as he hobbled away into the bustle of the city.

Ezra walked without thinking through the tiny cobbled streets of the Île de la Cité. Lawyers in their black robes thronged the streets, and he realized he was close by the Palais de Justice. Outside were pinned the notices of trials and sentencing, times and places of execution. Something drew him to scan them for Loveday's name. Would it be there yet?

The names were too numerous, the times of execution now every other day. He pulled up short at *Anne Duchamp, seamstress* – she was dying tomorrow too. He forced himself to keep looking. There were people from Paris, from Brittany, from Bordeaux, from Poitiers, from Gascony like Luc. All of France was here, it seemed.

And yes, *Loveday Finch*; her only designation: *English*. Tomorrow, with Anne Duchamp in the Place de Grève, where the diligence had arrived, where he had first stepped down into this city. At noon. Ezra's breath caught. A mere twenty-three hours left of breathing, of heartbeats, of life.

He looked away. He could see the roofs of the Conciergerie through the jumble of buildings ahead. Ezra was suddenly and very violently sick – passers-by gave him a wide berth as he bent over and emptied his stomach, but nobody stopped for him. He straightened up, dazed. What little chance there had been for Loveday's life lay in the gutter along with his vomit.

He turned and tried to run. He didn't want to go back to the little house, he didn't want to be here, in this city, in this place any more. He needed to think, but his head was buzzing. Luc and Mahmoud would be on their way to Le Havre right now. Ezra tried to imagine telling them the whole story and had to stop again. "Idiot!" he shouted aloud at himself. Maybe the best that he could hope for was for someone to finish the job that the warder at the Conciergerie had begun: to beat him to a pulp here, and fling him into the Seine from the Pont Neuf.

He stopped midway across the bridge and looked down at the sluggish grey water. Behind him were the Île de la Cité, Notre-Dame, the Hôtel-Dieu and the Conciergerie. Ahead, the slaughterhouses and tanneries spilt their blood and fat into the cold river. The crowds around took no notice. He was just a black boy with a swollen face. The pamphleteers strode up and down, pushing past, shouting the news. This was the longed-for revolution, where girls – no, where anyone who opened their mouth – was subjected to summary violence and nobody cared for anything any longer.

That was when he heard it, one of the pamphleteers yelling in a sing-song voice, "General Dumas awarded medal for bravery!"

Ezra turned towards the sound. There were at least three other small boys calling other news, and he thought he must have imagined it. He stepped away from the edge, picked up his bag. *General* Dumas?

He listened harder, pushing his way into the crowd until he heard the name again. He put on a burst of speed, his pain forgotten as he caught up with the boy, who looked startled by his urgency as much as by his swollen face. He held out his pamphlets anyway. "Latest news from the battlefield, *monsieur*?" he said, a little uncertainly.

"Yes – yes, thank you," panted Ezra. He handed the boy a couple of *sous* and shook out the paper. *Dumas,*

General Commander of the American Regiment. Fêted for the capture of an entire Hapsburg regiment of sixty fighting Netherlanders with a platoon of only fourteen.

He remembered the last pamphlet he'd read about Dumas, at the house at the Rue des Lauriers, in which the man had been derided. And what was it Le Brun had said about their duel – the end of his regiment? But now here he was a hero! And although there was nothing on this pamphlet to give the man's whereabouts – Ezra read it three times just to make sure – it was quite possible he could still be here in the city.

If there was anyone who could possibly help him now it would be Lieutenant Colonel – *General*, he corrected himself – Dumas. Maybe all was not lost.

Ezra folded the pamphlet carefully, put it in his pocket, and made his way off the bridge to the Quai de la Mégisserie to hail a cab. The first few didn't stop, and as they trotted away, Ezra shouted after them the French curses Luc had used.

Eventually a shabby cab with a tired horse and a wary driver pulled up in front of him.

"War Office, please!" Ezra called as he climbed aboard.

The ride was bumpy and uncomfortable, made worse by Ezra's anxious impatience, but he thanked the driver all the same, and tipped him as well as he could afford to. He climbed out of the cab, limped up the steps, and begged to be let upstairs, or at least to have the General's Paris address. But the young man on the desk looked daggers at him and refused to let him past, would tell him nothing.

Ezra exploded. "Citizen Le Brun? Remember him?

I was here in his office only days ago! He was in a duel and I sewed him up!"

The clerk was unmoved.

"I was with the American Regiment – that day, the day Dumas captured all those prisoners."

The young man raised an eyebrow.

"You don't believe me? I am a surgeon, man!"

This time the man visibly smirked. Ezra looked up, catching sight of his reflection in the glass of a portrait hanging over the desk, and suddenly realized – of course he did not believe him. He saw for the first time what looked like a monster staring back at him. No wonder the cab hadn't stopped – no wonder the youth was smirking at him as if he'd just scraped himself off the street.

His face was misshapen, his jaw on the left side twice its natural size. His jacket was stained and filthy with blood. The instrument case looked incongruous, as if he had stolen it.

High on the wall was a massive ornate clock, all gold scrolls and curls. Its stiffly moving hands read three o'clock. Ezra's heart skipped a beat. This time tomorrow Loveday would be...

With fresh resolve, he lifted up his instrument case and slammed it down on the desk, clicked opened the lock. There, nestled in the bottle-green velvet, were his tools, clean and ready for use. The young man goggled. Ezra saw a flicker of fear. Very well, he thought. If I look like a monster, that is what I shall be.

"See?" he snarled. "These are my tools. Each one is a very old friend." He picked them up in turn and listed their names. "Bone saw. Hinged bone saw. Finger saw."

He lingered over the French names for the tools. The youth was recoiling. Good, Ezra thought.

"Flesh knives. Large, curved, small." The youth was pale. "Catlin knife. Artery hook. Forceps."

"Yes! All right! I believe you are a surgeon, but General Dumas is not here, I swear."

"Then you will tell me where he is staying. Quickly. I don't have time to wait around."

The young man took up his quill, scrawled out an address and pushed it warily across the desk. Ezra wanted to smile but reminded himself it would rather spoil the effect. Instead he snapped the box shut and leant close. He remembered the way Mr McAdam's last footman, Toms, had spoken, always low and slow and with a hint that violence was only a breath away. Ezra waited, watched the young man squirm. Leant closer.

"If you are lying, I will return, I promise, and perhaps introduce you to some more of my sharp, shiny friends."

The youth shook his head. He was terrified, there were beads of sweat on his brow. Ezra thought he would be useless in any kind of war, and that it was a good thing he had a desk job. Ezra could see he wasn't lying. He read the address – *Rue des Mathurins* – but it meant nothing. It could have been anywhere. He picked up his bag, saw the youth's shoulders droop with relief.

"One more thing." The youth nodded nervously. Ezra pushed the paper back. "Draw me a map."

Ezra stepped out into the street again, exhilarated. What had he just done? It was almost frightening how easily his inner bully had emerged. What had he said? *Sharp*, *shiny friends!* Loveday would never believe it when he told her.

He swallowed. First he had to get her out, and to do that he needed to find Dumas.

Ezra ended up hobbling the short distance from the War Office to the smart streets north of the Boulevard de la Madeleine. Here were large old houses, set back from the street. There were more trees here, too, pink cherry and white apple blossom drifting down over courtyard gardens. Ezra soon found the Rue des Mathurins, where Dumas was lodging.

It didn't take long to find the right house. Ezra knocked on the glossy black-painted door and the maid told him the tradesman's entrance was at the back. The old, mild Ezra would have backed off. This new monstrous Ezra scowled and put his foot in the door, and the maid screamed. From inside the house the sound of thunder turned out to be booted footsteps, and there, taking the stairs two at a time in his riding boots, sword hanging at his waist and clean-shaven now, was Dumas. He carried a hat in one hand and looked like a warrior stepped down from his horse in some painting or other. He appeared to have been preparing to leave, but the maid's scream had brought him running.

He stared at Ezra with a face like thunder, but all Ezra could do was sag with relief.

"Lieutenant Colonel! Thank heavens!" he said. He nodded a bow, and corrected himself, "I mean, sir, General."

"I ask no one to bow to me," Dumas said. He was frowning as he looked hard at Ezra. "McAdam? Is it you?" The general came close and stared at Ezra's swollen face. He smiled in recognition. "What in all heaven's name happened to you, man?"

"I need to talk to you, sir. I need to ask…"

At that moment a matched pair of black horses drew up, pulling a dark landau with the roof down. The driver nodded at Dumas, and Dumas took Ezra's hand and shook it.

"McAdam, it is good to see you. It breaks my heart to see what is happening in Paris, and the regiment –" he frowned again – "I would be lying if I said we were not in trouble."

"But you are a hero," said Ezra. "The papers are singing your name."

"A hero who fought a minister of the War Office." Dumas shook his head and picked up a pair of fine kid gloves from the hall table.

"Le Brun? I know – I sewed the man up."

"Ha! I would never have killed him. I just wanted to show him." Dumas sighed. "I should not have got angry like that. He would wipe the American Regiment off the face of the earth if he had his way."

The general stepped out into the road and Ezra followed. This conversation was not going the way he had imagined.

"Dumas, please! I am sorry, but I need to speak to you." Ezra cast a look at the maid hovering close by; she still looked nervous. "Alone. And urgently. It is my friend, remember? The girl I told you about. She is imprisoned falsely. She faces death." Ezra realized he must sound desperate.

Dumas smiled. "At your age, it is always a girl, I think. She is the magician you spoke of? It is a shame, then, that she cannot walk through walls." His face became serious. "The Conciergerie is a terrible place. The only people who come out of there are the dead, or those who are soon to be dead."

"Exactly, that's why—" Ezra began.

"I cannot talk now, my friend." General Dumas nodded to the waiting landau. "There are those who would disband the regiment, who spread lies about us. They hand out plaudits with one hand and stab you in the back with the other. I have an appointment with a committee of the National Convention concerning the fate of the regiment. They will not wait for me."

"But…" Ezra felt the world sinking beneath his feet. Dumas walked past him and climbed into the landau.

"Come for supper," Dumas called down. "We can talk then, Sawbones. I will expect you tomorrow. At eight!" He settled himself in the seat.

"But that's too late!" Ezra clung to the door of the landau. "I need your help, sir. There is no one else!" He felt something in his eye, a piece of grit perhaps.

Dumas looked him full in the face. "You told me about Loveday Finch and the Turk. Last year, you thought all was lost; you stood against the politics of two great states and still you succeeded." He put out an arm and rested it on Ezra's shoulder. "From what I have seen of you, young man, you will fight. The battle is not lost yet. Remember that." Dumas sat back in the landau and called out to the driver. *"Salle du Manège!"* The carriage set off at a smart trot.

Ezra stood in the road and wiped his face. If Dumas believed in him, then maybe…

"Tomorrow, at eight!" he called to the back of the landau as it rounded the corner into the wide boulevard and sped away.

Behind him the maid slammed the door hard, and the street was quiet again.

As he stumbled back to the main highway to find a cab he heard a clock strike for four. Loveday had twenty hours. Ezra had no idea how, but this time tomorrow, he told himself, Loveday would be free.

Chapter Fifteen

Rue des Lauriers
Near Saint-Sulpice
Paris
31 March 1793

Ezra reached the Rue des Lauriers with no idea of how he would achieve his goal. The man in the dairy on the corner saw him coming and rushed out with a cheese fresh from Normandy, which he pressed on him free of charge.

"Your friend, the *mademoiselle* with the red hair, she was brave," the dairyman said. "She barely knew our Laurent, and still she tried to save him."

He'd never passed two words with the fellow, yet he was all kindness, even with Ezra wearing a blood-stained jacket and a ghoul's battered face. Ezra thanked him. He would change as soon as he got in, he told himself: clean shirt, clean mind.

The action made him think – people were kind, most people, even when life was so cheap. He had made a friend in the prison, hadn't he, the woman in the sick bay? She had been grateful for those few grains of lauda-num. He walked down the street towards the house with not quite a spring in his step but at least the seed of hope. There must be a way. He just had to think of it.

He went up the three steps to the door and froze. It was open – just a crack, but he could see the lock was broken, kicked in by the looks of it. Ezra stood on the threshold for a moment, fumbling with his instrument case – he needed a knife; whoever had broken in might still be there. He pushed the door open slowly and quietly.

"I am armed. I will hurt you." He used the same low voice that had terrified the clerk at the War Office. There was a small fire burning in the grate, and propped up in the chair, face whiter than starched linen, was Luc, his forehead slick with sweat. Ezra rushed inside.

"What in heaven's name! You were supposed to be in Le Havre!" He put a hand on the boy's forehead and turned down the blanket that had been tucked under his chin. "You're burning up. Luc! Luc?"

Luc made no reply. Ezra checked his pulse; it was racing, thumping like a horse cantering on a cobbled street. His breathing was shallow, and when Ezra lifted his eyelids he saw his eyes had rolled back in his head. Ezra slapped Luc around the face. His eyelids seemed to flutter and he let out a low moan, but he didn't wake.

Ezra took off his jacket and bent down over the boy. "I'm going to take you upstairs, *d'accord*?"

The boy groaned again when Ezra picked him up, a good sign, Ezra thought, until the blanket slid to the floor and suddenly there was a sickly sweet smell of putrefaction. Ezra put Luc down again and prised off his boot. He stepped back. It was the foot, the limb was swollen and hot. The bandage around Luc's half-foot was stained with blood and pus. Ezra slowly and carefully peeled it back. What remained of Luc's foot was dying, the stitches tight against the bloated, decaying flesh.

Ezra sighed. "Oh, Luc, why didn't you say something?"

The boy didn't answer.

Ezra should have changed the dressing, should have made time to look at it before he'd sent them on their way to Le Havre, but he'd been too worried about Loveday. He groaned to himself. He was a fool! Loveday was awaiting death and Luc was already halfway to heaven. Ezra would have to operate, otherwise the infection would spread up the leg and surely kill him. The young surgeon looked round – he could lift him onto the dining table, he thought, worry about the mess afterwards.

Ezra went upstairs and fetched a pillow to put under Luc's head, and a sheet to tear into strips for bandages. When he came down he cleared the table, sweeping the pamphlets to the floor, and took the candlesticks and put them on the mantelpiece. He opened the shutters on the window. He needed light.

He turned round and almost jumped a foot. There was Mahmoud carrying a jug of water and a bag of shopping in from the street.

Mahmoud stared. "By all the names! What happened to your face?"

"This? It's nothing." Ezra paused. "You were supposed to get on the boat! You were supposed to be safe!"

"Luc was ill. I am neither stupid nor callous."

Ezra calmed a little. "No, of course not."

"I had to bring him here. What else could I do?" Mahmoud's expression was sombre, but there was a hint of fear as he asked, "Is he very ill?"

"I think so."

Mahmoud swallowed, but he steeled himself and nodded. "You will fix him?"

"I cannot promise anything. There are two things wrong with him now, his lower leg has necrotized."

Mahmoud made a face.

"The flesh is rotting, as far as the ankle," Ezra explained. "On top of that he has a fever. Either could kill him. I can only treat the leg and hope Luc is strong enough to recover from the operation and the fever."

"Couldn't you wait?" Mahmoud asked. "Until the fever has passed?"

"I cannot say which will kill him quicker," Ezra said gravely.

Mahmoud looked at him. "Well," he said, "I will help you move him. And Loveday, she is safe now?"

Ezra looked away. "One thing at a time, Mahmoud." He picked up his instrument case. "We have an operation to perform, and I will need an assistant. Luc is away with the fever but no doubt he'll feel the blade of my saw."

"I bought some rum with the last of our cash."

"Good. Let's to work."

They tried to wake Luc enough that he could swallow some of the spirits, but he was already deeply unconscious. Ezra set him down on the table as gently as he could.

"Make him live," Mahmoud said as he arranged the pillow under his friend's head. He sounded as commanding and matter of fact as ever, but Ezra could tell a plea when he heard one. Mahmoud stared at Luc's slick, stinking, swollen ankle, and Ezra saw his eyes widen.

"He never said it was that bad! He never complained about the pain at all, and then he fainted, just as we arrived at Le Havre. He became delirious on the way back to Paris. As we passed the outer wall, the one they are pulling down, he lost consciousness. I had to carry him back to the house."

Ezra gave the diseased limb one more look. He could cut just above the ankle, but the infection might remain.

"It's best," he said, "if I take it off above the knee."

Mahmoud made a face. "So much?"

Ezra didn't say aloud that the young French boy's chances were still very slim. That the procedure was kill or cure. That Luc might never wake up again. He turned to Mahmoud. "Find something for Luc to bite on if he wakes, and be ready to hold him still. That is imperative. If he wakes, you must ensure his leg does not move."

Mahmoud looked at Luc's unconscious form. "I doubt if anything much would wake him."

He was right, but Ezra thought it better Mahmoud was occupied.

"Do it," Ezra said, "please. But first we need a tourniquet."

Ezra tore a sheet and tied it tightly around Luc's thigh. He pulled as hard as he could. Luc did not twitch as the tourniquet bit hard into his skin.

"This will stop the blood flow," Ezra explained. Mahmoud said nothing but looked on, his eyes large and round in his small face.

Ezra closed his eyes for a second and imagined himself back in the operating theatre at St Bartholomew's. The smell of sawdust and rosemary from the cutting floor, the cloud of good pipe tobacco from the audience. He took out his sharpest flesh knife, and under his breath he began to count.

"One," Ezra murmured as he made his first incision into the healthy skin above Luc's knee.

Mahmoud swallowed nervously and pressed his whole weight down on Luc's upper thigh above the tourniquet.

Ezra cut through the top layer of skin and into the flesh around the bone. He frowned; the boy had not moved, he was – no, he wouldn't think it.

"Luc, you will not die!" he cried aloud.

Mahmoud leant close to Luc's pallid face, panicked. "I, Mahmoud of the house of Othman, order you to live!"

Ezra took the larger knife and cut through what little muscle there was to expose the bone. Blood was everywhere, he hastily wiped it on his jacket and reached for the bone saw. He needed to be quick, he needed to close up as soon as he was done.

Mahmoud saw the bone and his mouth dropped open. He was watching Ezra closely now. "Will you sew him up?"

"I don't think so, I've left enough of a skin flap."

"We are animals, all of us, underneath," Mahmoud murmured, only just audible over the sawing.

Luc's diseased leg fell onto the floor and Ezra quickly and deftly flapped over the skin, then wiped his hands and began to pack and bandage the wound.

"He will wake up, won't he?"

"We must hope so," Ezra said.

Mahmoud's gaze dropped to the floor, and he nodded as he let out a shaky breath. Ezra could see him pulling himself together. "Tell me about Loveday," he said. "She is still in prison?"

Ezra concentrated on bandaging the stump as neatly as he could so that he wouldn't have to look at Mahmoud.

"It's worse than that. She is to go to the guillotine tomorrow. At noon." Ezra related what had happened with Renaud at the Conciergerie, and how he had failed to enlist Dumas's help. Then he bound and tied the end of the bandage. "General Dumas said I could do it alone, and you know, for a moment I thought I could."

Mahmoud looked at him. "Only for a moment? Are you quite mad?"

Ezra looked back at the boy, raised an eyebrow, tucked in the end of the bandage.

Mahmoud studied the remains of the leg on the floor, frowning. His shoulders were tense.

"Of course Loveday Finch will not die," he said firmly. "I am the son of the sultan and I will not have it. I am very determined."

"Mahmoud, Loveday's prison is impenetrable; the walls are high; the cart to the guillotine is guarded."

"There are no buts. You have saved Luc's life."

Ezra opened his mouth. He was about to say that Luc's life was very far from saved. That he might still die today, tomorrow, next week. Mahmoud put up his hand to stop him.

"If you can do that, you can easily save another. Take me to the prison and we will find a way."

"Mahmoud, you forget, they know my face, both the face I had before I was beaten up and this one. They will not let me in."

"Enough!" Mahmoud's lower lip was trembling, but he was resolute. "I have willed it," he insisted. "It will come to pass! And what is more, I have the gun – we will go there now. Luc is asleep, and by the looks of him he will not miss us." Mahmoud was staring at Ezra now, his fists clenched. "I shall bury this … leg. You shall clean yourself up. Then you will walk with me and we will fashion Loveday's escape from prison and Paris."

Mahmoud had not stopped plotting all the way along the Rue de Sevres, each scheme more ridiculous and unworkable than the next. Ezra threw a stone into the sluggish grey water of the Seine and looked up at the towers of the Conciergerie.

Mahmoud was still talking. It was his eighth attempt at a plan, and he was growing more and more desperate. "And then we poison the cart driver and scare the horses, halfway to the Place – they bolt, and when I stop the cart you take the gun, kill the guard and drag Loveday off the back."

Ezra shook his head. "That will not work either. The guard on the cart will see me take aim and I will fall down dead."

Mahmoud wasn't giving up. "You said Loveday and Madame Lascelles engineered a riot?"

"They had the entire cast of the Cirque-Olympique in the crowd. And Renaud told me the militia regularly fire upon the crowd now. They will not risk a repeat."

Mahmoud sighed in frustration, and threw a stone into the water too.

Ezra had put on his old jacket. He felt in the pocket

– there were the handkerchiefs Loveday had vanished and changed over and over for the children outside the War Office.

He shook them out, one bright red silk as fluid as blood, another a blue as dark as the sky at night. He passed them from hand to hand, remembering how he'd spent hours learning to magically change one into another, from red to navy and back again. What was it Dumas had said?

"That it was a shame Loveday Finch could not walk through walls," Ezra spoke aloud, "because the only people who come out of that place are the dead, or those who are almost dead."

Mahmoud looked at him. "What did you say, McAdam?"

The clock at Notre-Dame struck for six. Ezra held the blood-red silk square up in front of Mahmoud, and shook it out. Instantly it seemed to vanish and change before his eyes to navy blue. Ezra smiled. "I think I might have had an idea."

Chapter Sixteen

Pont Saint-Michel
Île de la Cité
Paris
1 April 1793

It was dawn. The shops that lined the bridge were still closed. Ezra thought the city was beautiful, the sky streaked with lilac and pink and the air clear and clean, the rooftops and steeples and domes reaching up to the sky like so many hopes and dreams rendered in stone and tiles. The ghost of the moon hung in the sky too, and Ezra made a child's wish that all would go well.

He could see the Conciergerie clearly from here. It stood just beyond the old palace that had been built for a prince, and its grim circular towers, black with five hundred years of dirt, soared above the Hôtel-Dieu. Ezra picked up his skirts carefully and walked on.

He had never realized just how heavy dresses were. He supposed he had a deal of items in his pockets, but even so, with all the skirts and underskirts it was like wearing half a laundry cupboard. He had on an old blue dress of Loveday's, which was only a little too short but seemed to be flapping around his calves. He reminded himself to be grateful it no longer hurt to walk, and that the pain in his ribs and torso had somewhat decreased. In fact he thought the bodice of the dress, laced very close if not tight exactly – he was a deal broader than Loveday – seemed to act like a support. He pulled the hood of his cloak forward as a cart headed past him towards the south. Mahmoud had warned him he made a most unconvincing girl; his face was, the prince had told him, quite unpleasant in a variety of ways. Ezra felt the swelling. It still hurt and he imagined it would take a week or so to go down.

Mahmoud should have delivered all his messages by now and be on his way back to watch over Luc. The boy had not had a good night, still in a kind of deep unconsciousness even though his leg was free from infection. Ezra had not told Mahmoud he didn't know if the French boy would shake the fever, if he would ever regain consciousness. He shook the thought away. He had too much to think about, too much to do today. He had done all he could for poor Luc.

Ezra heard a clock chime for six. The plan was in motion now. If Mahmoud had played his part, the Hôtel-Dieu would send the cart for the bodies at eight. Ezra had two hours.

He reached the open square in front of the prison and took a little time to study the map Marie Durant had drawn for him the night before when he had waylaid her on the way home from work. Her daughter had at last had a better night's sleep with the assistance of the laudanum, and Madame Durant had been most helpful.

The map showed the sickroom and the various

staircases, as well as the oubliettes deep in the basements where prisoners who could not afford better were kept before their appointment with the guillotine. Ezra slowed, pulled the bonnet under his hood closer, and reminded himself to keep his eyes to the ground and speak as little as possible.

There was a huddle of people still waiting for news of relatives asleep round a little fire they had built against the wall. Ezra shuffled around to the door by the main gate and knocked.

He listened as the bolt slid back and a man in a revolutionary cap looked him up and down.

Ezra took a deep breath. He only had to say the one line: "Madame Durant is ill, I am her cousin, Hélène, come to take her duties on the ward for today." His voice wavered and wobbled, the register rising and falling most unconvincingly, he feared.

The man said nothing for a long time. Ezra could not fail on this first hurdle. He could not. Time seemed to have slowed. What in heaven's name was he doing? Ezra resisted the urge to look up. Then he heard the door open wide and he shuffled inside.

As he walked through the arch into the courtyard he heard the man shout after him, "Tell your cousin to send a pretty one next time!"

Ezra didn't look back, just hurried over to the staircase that led to the sick bay. When he reached it he almost collapsed, his legs weak with relief. It had worked – he was here.

The prison was still only half awake. A lone stable boy carried water for a couple of horses who stood heavy-lipped and droopy-mouthed in stalls built up against the wall. A farmer's tumbril, the one they used to take the prisoners to meet their destiny, lay shafts down, ready for its load.

Renaud had told him the Conciergerie had been built as a palace, long ago. Much like the Tower of London, it was hard to imagine a place so bleak and hard had ever been sumptuous, luxurious. Ezra hesitated just a moment, then began to climb up the stairs to the sick bay. Would the warders recognize him as the young surgeon they had seen only a day ago? He hoped not.

He took the key Marie Durant had given him out of his pocket and opened the door. Inside there was only one warder, and he was asleep in his chair by the ashes of the fire. He was snoring, and Ezra took quiet tiptoe steps across the floor, heading straight for Juliette's bed, when one of the other patients called out.

"Marie? Is that you? Water, I beg you, *J'ai soif.*"

The warder didn't wake. Ezra made his way over and found an almost empty jug on the floor. The patient, a young man who looked like a living skeleton, sat up with difficulty, and Ezra filled a chipped beaker and helped him take a few sips, cradling his head and mopping the drips that fell from his mouth. Ezra looked across the room to the bed under the window that Juliette had shared. Were both she and the old woman still there? He thought so.

He laid the man down again and went to see – but Juliette had gone. There was only the aged crone, who lay wide awake and grinning. She clacked her toothless gums at Ezra.

Ezra felt his heart speed up. Without Juliette, the plan was over.

"Juliette is dead." The crone giggled. "Dead and a whole lifetime younger than me." Ezra's heart sank. Juliette was not supposed to be dead. Not yet! He had brought with him more than enough laudanum to send her into oblivion. He was at least relieved that the responsibility for her death no longer rested on his shoulders, but without Juliette Durant's body he could not effect Loveday's escape. Ezra blinked. All was lost.

Across the room the warder snorted and snuffled in his sleep.

Ezra steadied himself against the wall. He would not give up now. "When did she die?" he asked.

"If you are a woman, I am Marie Antoinette." The old woman chuckled.

Ezra stepped back, the crone was laughing louder now, rolling on the bed. She was clearly mad. The warder was waking, then there was the sound of a door rattling.

Ezra cursed. He took a broom that was propped against the wall and, head bowed, began to sweep as if his life depended on it.

"Pierre!" It was another warder, broad as two of Ezra. He slapped his fellow awake by the fire. "Pierre, you lazy bastard," the man called.

Pierre stretched and yawned. "Tell that crazy old bird to shut up before I tie a knot in her throat."

The old woman stopped laughing suddenly. Ezra kept sweeping. Perhaps he could sneak out unnoticed.

Pierre stood up. "That kid snuffed it last night."

"Don't blame her," the other warder said. "I'd send

myself to the guillotine rather than share a bed with Gummy. Where'd you put her, or have you cleared her out already?"

Ezra stopped sweeping.

"I left her under the bed. Didn't have the strength to carry her all the way down to the sluice."

Ezra felt a wave of relief. He bent down, and there she was, wrapped in a dirty bedsheet, next to the pot. Marie Durant's daughter, and Loveday Finch's ticket out of jail. He wished he could murmur a thank you, to poor Juliette, to whatever providence had seen to it that her body had not yet been removed, but he could not risk being heard by the warders.

Ezra checked for rigor mortis as best he could through the bedsheet – it had not quite set in, for which he was thankful. Of course, he still had to find a way to carry her out past those two. He straightened up and swept harder. He stole a glance at the warders, one was building up the fire, the other was unwrapping some bread and cheese. He had an idea. These men must carry bodies up and down all the time. Why not let them do the work they were paid for? He cleared his throat. "Citizen Warders," he said, trying to pitch his voice higher. "How am I to sweep with this dead girl in the way?"

Half an hour later, Ezra was wheeling Juliette Durant along by the castle walls around the courtyard in a wheelbarrow. He apologized for heaping her with straw, and made his way quickly, but not so fast as to draw attention. After all, he was a man wearing a dress pushing a dead body in a wheelbarrow, and the place was getting busy.

Two stableboys were cleaning out the horses, telling jokes as if it was just another day, and there was the occasional sob or moan of prisoners all around. The prison clock struck for seven. Ezra kept wheeling. Only one hour left.

Marie Durant had told him about the oubliettes. They were the deepest dungeons in the prison, and in the past, she said, before the revolution, people were shut in there and forgotten, left to waste away and die before they had a chance to be hanged or guillotined. That's where Loveday was right now, awaiting the cart that would take her to her death at noon.

It was easy to find the staircase; Ezra followed his nose down and down round the spiral stairs, now carrying Juliette over his shoulder. She was light as a feather, nothing but skin and bone. He stumbled; the deeper he went, the darker it became. When he finally reached the bottom it was as dark as night.

"Excuse me, *mademoiselle*," Ezra whispered as he slid the body of Juliette off his shoulder and leant her gently against a wall. He could hear sounds up ahead. The air here was so thick with the smell of damp and excrement that he covered his mouth with his hand.

Around the corner was a long corridor. At the end of it he could see the orange glow of a fire and an elderly man poking at it with a stick. Ezra pressed himself against the wall. He knew what he had to do.

Marie had said the warder's name here was Michel. Ezra adjusted his dress and took out a flask. He stepped over Juliette and out into the light, flask in hand.

"Michel?" he cooed.

The laudanum seemed to take an age to work on the

man. Ezra tried to keep his voice girlish as he regaled the warder with Luc's best chicken jokes. By the time he'd got to the one about the goat and the side of mutton, Michel was drooling, mouth open, forehead resting on the dirty flagstones. Ezra unclipped his keys and went to fetch Juliette.

He ran up and down the cells, looking in, but each was darker and more fetid than the next, and he could only make out the dregs of inmates, barely stirring inside.

"*Anglaise!* English girl!" Ezra said, making his voice loud and harsh, hoping he sounded warder-like.

There was some muttering from the cells, then, at last, a voice.

"Who's asking?" It was Loveday. Her voice was weak but defiant. Ezra smiled, and, gently laying Juliette over his shoulder, opened the cell with the keys he'd taken from the warder.

All he could see of Loveday were the whites of her eyes, but he would know that voice anywhere.

"Loveday, it's me."

"*Ezra?*" He smiled and hugged her hard. "Ezra, thank heavens…"

"Don't talk," he whispered. "This is Juliette – she has come to help me save you. Dress her in your clothes while I keep watch."

Loveday gasped. "Ezra, she's dead!"

"I know," he hissed. "And you must pretend to be!" He untied a parcel from under his skirts. "Put this on. Quickly! And your boots, you'll have to take them off."

Loveday shook her head. "I sold them for stew the first night I was in here."

Ezra squeezed her hand.

Loveday didn't need telling twice.

She was, mercifully, the only one in her cell – Ezra didn't know what he would have done had that not been the case. He waited outside with the winding sheet, the one Juliette had been wrapped in, and in seconds Loveday came out, dressed in a nightshirt that reached her knees, pale and trembling in the dark but with that determined glint in her eyes that Ezra knew so well.

Ezra took a moment to bid farewell to Juliette. He hadn't needed to do for her what he had promised her mother, but at least he would be able to tell Marie that her daughter was at peace. Then he locked her into Loveday's cell and tied the keys back onto the warder, and finally led Loveday back down the corridor and up the stairs.

They stopped at the door to the courtyard and looked out. The wheelbarrow had gone – some useful boy must have taken it away. Oh well, he'd have to do without it. Ezra couldn't see the Conciergerie clock. He had no idea how long they had.

He turned back to Loveday, who was squinting in the light, not used to the morning sun after being locked up in the dark. Under a layer of filth her face was pale as a ghost, her red hair matted and sticking up in clumps. Ezra took his apron and wiped her face.

"If Mahmoud was successful, the wagon from the Hôtel-Dieu will arrive at eight. They put the bodies of dead prisoners next to the laundry by the sluice. I will wrap you in this sheet and take you there."

The sheet was disgusting, stained with excrement, but

Loveday nodded and gratefully wrapped herself in it as if it was a silken gown made for royalty.

Ezra wound the end of the sheet around her, then slung her up across his shoulder and walked purposefully towards the sluice.

He was not stopped. He could not believe his luck. He shut the door of the small stone room hard behind him. It was dark inside, but his eyes soon acclimatized. There were two bodies there already. One was stiff – dead yesterday, Ezra thought – the other fresher. He took out his needle and thread to sew Loveday into the sheet, and looked at the three bundles. Loveday's was breathing. The movement of her chest, up and down, was too obvious. He held her hand through the cloth. She was obviously warm. Too warm. He unwrapped her and helped her to stand.

"You are too warm and you are breathing. If you breathe and they see it, you will be dead. Do you hear me?"

"I am as good as dead," Loveday said. Ezra felt his stomach somersault, she sounded so un-Loveday-like, so empty and drained. So close to giving up her hold on life. He swallowed, held her head so she could not look away.

"Listen to me! You will not die here! We have to make this work." He fetched a pail of cold water from the laundry and washed her down, doused her hands and feet, mopped her face and forehead.

"I don't think," Loveday said, smiling faintly despite the chattering of her teeth, "I could be any less alive than this."

She was standing, dripping, on the stone floor. He

could see her toes were black and blue with cold and dirt and bruises.

"We will get you out of here," he promised. "Just don't shiver."

As Ezra tied off the thread, he heard a clock somewhere strike for eight. He looked at the shape of Loveday under the sheet, and leant close to her head. "When they come for you, hold your breath and lie limp. Completely limp. I will see you in the morgue of the Hôtel-Dieu." Ezra opened the door a crack and could see people coming. "Good luck, my friend," he said, and ducked away into the laundry.

The wagon was only a few minutes late. The wagoners reversed it up to the sluice and, deep in discussion about last night's dog fight, threw the three bundles into the back so carelessly that Ezra thought he might not have bothered trying to make Loveday's feigned death so convincing.

Ezra stood in the courtyard, shielding his eyes from the sun, and watched as they opened the main gates and the wagon lurched out. He didn't realize he had been holding his breath until it had gone.

He could have danced. Instead, before he could turn around, one of the stableboys bumped into him with a barrowful of manure and it went up into the air and all over Ezra's dress.

The boy looked terrified, due for a slap, but Ezra could not have cared less. To the boy's amazement, Ezra kissed him square on the forehead, and dusted himself down. Time to leave.

Up at the gate he could see the gatekeeper distracted, petitioned by a wealthy man with a basket of food. Ezra walked slowly and evenly towards the entrance, held up his key, and carried on out through the gate. He kept walking just long enough to be out of sight, then he picked up his skirts and ran to the Hôtel-Dieu. He felt so ecstatic he thought his lungs would burst. Loveday was out of prison! She might be stacked on the back of a wagon with a couple of dead bodies, but she was free.

Ezra skidded around the corner, down a couple of alleys too narrow for a cart to pass, and reached the Hôtel-Dieu in time to see the wagon rolling inside. He put on a turn of speed and ran in behind it. The gate-keeper shouted, but when he saw it was Ezra, and in a dress, he laughed incredulously and waved him through, shouting after him that he wanted to hear the story later.

"You will, *je vous le promets!*" Ezra called back. He didn't doubt the man would hear it, but if everything went according to plan then Ezra would be a long way away by the time he did.

Ezra followed the wagon and watched as it turned left, away from the morgue and towards the main hospital building. He almost shouted to the wagoners, but then, standing in the road, was Renaud, red-faced, sleeves rolled up, already wearing his leather apron.

"*Imbéciles!*" Renaud exploded at the drivers. "I wanted the bodies for yesterday! I had to reschedule the entire demonstration!"

The wagoners rolled their eyes and pulled the horse to a stop.

"Come on then, now, there is no time to waste. The students are waiting!"

And before Ezra could stop them, the men had

unloaded two of the bodies, including the one that was Loveday, and carried them into the operating theatre. A scattering of medical students who looked as if they had only just woken up leant against the wooden rails smoking, a few with notebooks out.

Ezra tried to follow but Renaud blocked his way. *"Mademoiselle,"* he began, "this is a demonstration of the human body. I am not sure…"

Ezra tore off his bonnet.

Renaud did a double take.

"McAdam?" The Frenchman looked horrified. "What is the meaning of this? McAdam, what are you…?"

The students behind them were murmuring; there was some nervous laughter. Then someone gave a shout of alarm. Ezra looked past Renaud and immediately saw why: the cadaver on the dissection table had sat up inside its sheet. A couple of students began to scramble for the doors. Then there was a loud tearing sound and from inside the sheet Loveday emerged, blue-white and deathly cold, the sheet caught on her head like a veil. She could have been an avenging angel from a German woodcut. Renaud backed away in shock. The wagoners saw Loveday emerge from the winding sheet, and in a blaze of profanity dropped the other body and ran out of the operating theatre. Ezra took the opportunity to push past the French surgeon and run into the room.

"Loveday, come on!" he said, untying his cloak and putting it around her shoulders.

"Loveday – Loveday Finch?" Renaud said, staring. "But you were for the guillotine. Are you dead?"

Loveday fastened the cloak, the ghost of a smile hovering

about her blue-tinged lips. "I believe not, citizen."

"Get out of the way, man." Ezra realized his words probably lost some of their force given that he was wearing a dress. He turned to Loveday. She was smiling, properly now. "Mahmoud will be waiting for us."

"You are not going anywhere!" Renaud held a flesh knife in front of him like a weapon, his eyes flashing with fury. "I will not have it. You can both go back to the Conciergerie and the governor will thank me for it."

Ezra stepped forward. "I'm not afraid of you, Citizen Renaud. You're a butcher and a coward. You might have a surgeon's skills but you care nothing for the people it is your duty to help. Do you know what he planned, Loveday? Shall I tell you about his experiments? Drilling holes into prisoners' heads, looking for the centre of consciousness in live subjects..."

Loveday was speechless.

Renaud took his chance. He slashed at Ezra with his knife, cutting the fabric of the bodice. Ezra was unhurt, the blade had not reached the stays. Perhaps there were advantages to women's clothing after all.

Loveday was staring at Renaud. "Live people? You were going to cut open live people?"

"Only prisoners!" Renaud snapped. "All those sentenced to death—"

Loveday spun round as if she really was an avenging angel. She seized the Catlin knife from Renaud's medical kit and, lunging and parrying as if it was her own rapier, she disarmed the surgeon in a couple of swift strokes.

Renaud moaned. There was a cut opening up on his forearm.

Loveday was not sympathetic. "I expect you'll find it hurts less than a hole in the head."

"I will not let you get away," Renaud breathed.

Loveday leant forward and held the knife hard to his throat. "I think you will." Her knuckles were white.

Renaud went pale. He didn't reply. Loveday dropped the knife back into the instrument case and turned to the stunned medical students to give a deep bow.

"Loveday, come on!" Ezra hissed, and he took her hand and dragged her into the grounds and out of the gates. The morning rush had begun, and people and wagons crowded the Notre-Dame bridge, but there was no sign of Mahmoud. Ezra scanned the crowd. "He must be here. He must!"

"Can't we just take a cab?" Loveday said.

Ezra gave her a look. "Oh yes, a man in a dress and a girl who looks like death warmed up? They will turn us away, and we will be walking to Le Havre; Renaud will send a platoon of the National Guard to pluck us up and lock us away."

"You are such a misery sometimes!"

Then, all of a sudden, a smart landau drawn by two matched bays drew up in front of Ezra and Loveday on the cobbles, and the door opened. Inside sat General Dumas, smiling broadly.

"Your small Mediterranean friend was most insistent. He told me I must meet you here." Dumas looked from Ezra to Loveday and back. "Is this the famous Loveday Finch? And why, Friend McAdam, are you wearing a dress?" The general looked puzzled. "Am I late?"

Chapter Seventeen

Ezra was breathless, the anxiety in his chest only just beginning to recede. "I – we – cannot thank you enough," he said as the landau made its way south through the morning traffic towards the Pont Saint-Michel. General Dumas nodded.

"You needn't have come yourself, sir. It was just your landau," Ezra added, suddenly nervous of the tall, imposing man.

Dumas looked serious. "There are checkpoints all the way around the city on what is left of the old Farmer's Wall. One look at you in your dress and they might turn the horses round and send you back – but they won't stop me." He sat back in his seat, looking at Ezra with a wry smile. "I take it you succeeded."

Ezra nodded. "Only just."

The carriage had safely crossed over from the Île de la Cité and was set for the Rue des Lauriers before Ezra could fully relax. A smile spread across his face, and Loveday ran a hand through her filthy hair and smiled back. She was missing a tooth, just before her right upper canine, and her freckled face was pale, but she was somehow magnificent, radiant. Ezra began to laugh, nervously at first and then relieved, exhausted laughter – Dumas couldn't help joining in.

Ezra wiped his eyes on his flapping sleeves, and looked out of the window as the carriage whistled along the Rue de Sèvres.

"*You* laughing at *me*?" Loveday exclaimed. "Man in a dress! That was one of my favourites, and you have quite ruined it."

Ezra gave her a broad smile. "I promise never again to wear your clothes and never to break into another prison."

Dumas leant forward and looked at the pair of them. "So what in all heaven's name have you been up to?"

"General," Ezra said, "I could not begin to explain."

"What?" Loveday said. "That the celebrated anatomist and London surgeon, dressed all the while as a most unconvincing girl, effected the most audacious escape of the century?"

"Loveday," Ezra protested, "I assure you, however much of a friend you are, if you should make it known that I spent even five minutes looking like this…"

Loveday giggled. "Your secret is safe with me." She turned to Dumas. "This morning, sir, I was in the darkest dungeons of the Conciergerie."

Dumas's eyes widened. "In the oubliettes? *Mon dieu!*"

Loveday nodded. "I have died and been reborn."

"And then fought a duel," Ezra added, "with a surgeon's knife."

Dumas studied them both. "This sounds like the tallest tale I ever heard."

229

"Wait till he tells you about how we defeated a Russian spy!" Loveday said.

"Loveday, this is a gentleman whose life is more colourful than any of our exploits. He was abandoned, his mother sold in slavery, then he became a marquis and the bravest of the queen's own dragoons, and a general in the Revolutionary Army who – and I witnessed this with my own eyes – rode into battle and captured a whole Hapsburg company with one platoon of men. He is a real, honest-to-goodness hero. He doesn't want to hear about us!"

"On the contrary, I think I do." Dumas sighed. "If, as it seems, the regiment has been disbanded, then I will need some other tales to tell my children."

When they reached the house in the Rue des Lauriers Mahmoud was waiting for them at the door, his solemn face for once open and smiling. "Luc! Luc has opened his eyes! I have been waiting hours to tell you!"

Ezra scrambled out of the landau and rushed inside. Luc was sitting up, still pale but his temperature closer to normal.

He looked at Ezra, groggy but sharp-eyed. "I thought it couldn't get any worse than losing my foot, and now you have taken off the rest of my leg to go with it! How am I to be any good to anyone like this?"

Ezra shook his head with a weary smile. "You will return to London with me, Luc – didn't I promise?" What would his housekeeper Mrs Boscaven make of a one-legged French boy – the enemy – sitting in her kitchen, drinking hot chocolate? He would talk her round, he decided – and if he could not, then he was sure it would not take long for Luc to pick up enough English to win her over himself. Mahmoud had been right: he owed the boy a new start.

"Have you something in your eye?" Luc asked as Ezra and Mahmoud helped him out to the carriage.

"No, not at all. It's nothing," Ezra said, setting him down next to Loveday, who hugged the boy tightly.

"Who's this?" Luc exclaimed as he caught sight of General Dumas. "Your father, American? I never saw such fancy boots in my life!"

Mahmoud helped Ezra bring the rest of the luggage out from the house. Loveday was reunited with her sword, which impressed Dumas; they talked avidly of duelling, and Ezra had to warn her to keep the sword sheathed in the crowded carriage.

Luc, his spirits lifted with the promise of a fine new boot for his remaining foot and all the buns he could eat, told some more execrable jokes, and Ezra thought he had never felt so happy in his life. A wave of excitement and exhilaration coursed through his body. At last he would be going back to England. Back to London, to Great Windmill Street, where every jar in his laboratory would be just as he left it; where the church bells still rang, and nobody attempted to raise the dead.

Luc begged to hear the tale of the rescue in all its detail, and in his relief Ezra was only too glad to retell it. When he forgot some detail or other Loveday chipped in, and then Mahmoud began a highly coloured account of his kidnap, and the death of a Russian spy. Dumas listened keenly, and they were still talking when the landau pulled in outside the coaching inn at Poissy.

They were just finishing a very decent supper and Dumas had booked them all rooms, including one for himself; it was getting late. He would return to Paris in the morning, he said, then travel back to his wife, who lived with her family in a small town north-east of Paris.

"I swear your tales are more outlandish than any that one hears at military academy," he said as he put down his napkin. "Once, and I swear this is no lie, I fought three duels in one day. But I never killed an agent of a foreign empire in the catacombs! Tell me this is not some fancy woven from penny ballads?"

"On the contrary, sir," Ezra said. "I am afraid it is all true."

"You are more entertaining than the Paris Opera, and only slightly less dangerous," Dumas commented. "Perhaps you should set it down, write a book."

"Yes, Ezra, you should. And when I return to London I should be happy to read it."

"You *are* coming back then?" Ezra said, sounding uncertain in spite of himself.

"Of course! Stop being a misery, Ezra! You and Luc shall have all the fun, with your dead bodies and your anatomy school. Meanwhile Mahmoud will sit in splendour in a tiled palace."

"Not all of the time! Mahmoud scoffed. "But I shall keep those Russians at bay."

"There. And I will see you again. Eventually." Loveday pressed the hole in her gum. "I thought I could get a barber-surgeon in Constantinople to fix me a tooth made of quartz or somesuch. What do you think?"

Ezra shook his head. "I do not think such a thing is possible."

Loveday looked at the company sitting around the table. "Have you learnt nothing, Ezra McAdam? Look around you. A surgeon, a general –" she lowered her voice – "a prince, a beggar and a girl who was dead and still lives. From where I am sitting, everything is infinitely possible!"

Epilogue

Loveday and Mahmoud made it to Constantinople, where the valide sultan was so pleased to see her grandson alive that she endowed Loveday with a small fortune, half of which she sent to Ezra in London. Loveday spent an interesting year dressed as a boy learning new conjuring tricks from a Turkish maestro. She did not get a new tooth.

Ezra and Luc had to travel back to London via Dublin because of the war. It took the best part of a month and Ezra vowed never to leave London or his anatomy school ever again. Once back in Soho he bought Luc the finest silver-buckled shoe he could find. Ezra spent the next few years looking into the body's defences against infection and almost discovered the importance of cleanliness and antiseptics – or he would have done, except he refused to be parted from his lucky leather apron, which had belonged to Mr McAdam and was crusted with forty years of blood and worse.

Luc discovered the baker's in Lisle Street and developed a passion for Chelsea buns. He became very good at hopping and could be seen leading a crowd of boys in hopping races sweeping down Archer Street at a pace. He always won.

* * *

General Dumas is an incredible man in every way. For one, I did not make him up, his full name was Thomas-Alexandre Davy Dumas de la Pallieterie and he was a general in chief in the French Army during and after the revolution. You might not have heard of him, but I expect you know a lot more than you think.

Thomas Dumas was born into slavery on the island of San Domingue (now Haiti) in the Caribbean. His father was a marquis and his mother was a slave. When his father failed to make a massive fortune as a slave-owning planter he returned to France, but not before selling Thomas's mother and brothers and sisters. Thomas he merely abandoned, sending for him in 1776 and putting him through the top French military academy. Thomas was a great swordsman and a brilliant horseman, and when the revolution came he gave up his title and joined the army to fight for liberty, fraternity and equality. His feats of bravery on the battlefield became legend. He is still, today, the highest ranking man of African descent in a European army. He was over six foot tall and very gallant and dashing. When Napoleon led the French Army into Egypt, the Egyptians assumed General Dumas was their leader.

Ah, you say, he sounds interesting but *I've* never heard of him.

However, Thomas Dumas had a son who grew up to be the bestselling author in France, in Europe, in the world, for decades. There are still films made of his books, in fact the latest reincarnation of one of his best-loved tales is on British TV right now. Thomas's son was a little boy when his father died. He heard all the stories of bravery, strength and derring-do and thought he'd write a biography of his father, but it wasn't half as popular as the fiction based on these tales. Based on the swordsmanship and strength shown by his father. The son? Alexander Dumas. Those books? *The Three Musketeers*.

And if you were wondering where Alexander got the idea for the escape in *The Count of Monte Cristo*, maybe a young man he met told him a wild tale that happened once in Paris...

Acknowledgements

First of all, my massive thanks to Harry Catlin, whose help was invaluable. Harry, you made Ezra live and breathe his way around eighteenth-century Paris. This book would never have existed without you: my first reader, fiercest editor and super brilliant ideas merchant. I bow down.

And of course huge thanks to my lovely publishers at Walker, especially Emma Lidbury, who whipped the story into shape, and of course my agent, Stephanie Thwaites.

If you enjoyed this book, try these:

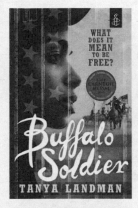

www.walker.co.uk

@WalkerBooksUK

CATHERINE JOHNSON is an award-winning writer of Welsh/African Caribbean descent, now living in Hastings in East Sussex. Her novels for children include *Stella*, *The Dying Game*, *Arctic Hero* and *A Nest of Vipers*, which was shortlisted for the UKLA Award. *Sawbones*, her first novel about Ezra McAdam and Loveday Finch, won the Historical Association's Young Quills Award for Historical Fiction, and *The Curious Tale of the Lady Caraboo* was shortlisted for the YA Book Prize.

Catherine also writes for film and TV, including *Holby City*, and her radio play *Fresh Berries* was nominated for the Prix d'Italia. She works regularly with children and teachers in primary schools and libraries across the UK. To find out more about Catherine and her writing, go to:

www.catherinejohnson.co.uk